Praise for
and her delightful H

"Rose Pressey
—New York Times b
Evanovich

IF YOU'VE GOT IT, HAUNT IT
"A delightful protagonist, intriguing twists, and a fashionista ghost combine in a hauntingly fun tale. Definitely haute couture."
—New York Times **best-selling author Carolyn Hart**

"If you're a fan of vintage clothing and quirky ghosts, Rose Pressey's *If You've Got It, Haunt It* will ignite your passion for fashion and pique your otherworldly interest. Wind Song, the enigmatic cat, adds another charming layer to the mystery."
—New York Times **best-selling author**
Denise Swanson

"*If You've Got It, Haunt It* is a stylish mystery full of vintage fashions and modern flair, with a dash of Rose Pressey's trademark paranormal wit for that final touch of panache. Chic and quirky heroine Cookie Chanel and a supporting cast of small-town Southern characters are sure to charm lovers of high fashion and murderous hi-jinks alike."
—New York Times **and** *USA Today* **best-selling author Jennie Bentley**

"Absolutely delightful! Prolific author Rose Pressey has penned a delightful mystery full of Southern charm, vintage fashion tips, a ghostly

presence, and a puzzler of a mystery. With snappy dialogue and well-drawn characters in a lovely small-town setting, this thoroughly engaging story has it all."
—*New York Times* **best-selling author Jenn McKinlay**

"Fun, fast-paced, and fashionable, *If You've Got It, Haunt It* is the first in Rose Pressey's appealing new mystery series featuring clever vintage-clothing expert Cookie Chanel. A charming Southern setting, an intriguing murder, a stylish ghost, a tarot-reading cat, and a truly delectable detective combine to make Ms. Pressey's new Haunted Vintage series a sheer delight."
—*New York Times* **best-selling author Kate Carlisle**

"Prolific mystery author Pressey launches a cozy alternative to Terri Garey's 'Nicki Styx' series with an appealing protagonist who is as sweet as a Southern accent. The designer name-dropping and shopping tips from Cookie add allure for shopaholics."
—*Library Journal*

IF THE HAUNTING FITS, WEAR IT
"Cookie Chanel must investigate the horse-racing community to find a killer. . . . After *Haunted Is Always in Fashion*, Pressey's fifth amusing paranormal cozy is filled with quirky characters and fashion, along with a few ghosts. Fans of Juliet Blackwell's 'Witchcraft' mysteries may enjoy the vintage clothing references. Suggest also for fans of Tonya Kappes."
—*Library Journal*

MURDER CAN MESS UP YOUR MASTERPIECE

Rose Pressey

KENSINGTON BOOKS
www.kensingtonbooks.com

KENSINGTON BOOKS are published by

Kensington Publishing Corp.
119 West 40th Street
New York, NY 10018

All Kensington titles, imprints, and distributed lines are available at special quantity discounts for bulk purchases for sales promotion, premiums, fund-raising, educational, or institutional use.

Special book excerpts or customized printings can also be created to fit specific needs. For details, write or phone the office of the Kensington Sales Manager: Attn.: Sales Department. Kensington Publishing Corp., 119 West 40th Street, New York, NY 10018. Phone: 1-800-221-2647.

First Printing: November 2019
ISBN-13: 978-1-4967-2161-7
ISBN-10: 1-4967-2161-6

ISBN-13: 978-1-4967-2162-4 (ebook)
ISBN-10: 1-4967-2162-4 (ebook)

10 9 8 7 6 5 4 3 2 1

Printed in the United States of America

*To my son, the kindest, most wonderful person
I've ever known.
He motivates me every day.
He's the love of my life.*

CHAPTER 1

Travel trailer tip 1:
When hooking up a travel trailer, remember to
watch out for the hitch.
Your shins will thank you.

With a pitch-black sky full of twinkling stars and a warm summer breeze caressing my skin, I stood in front of my fabulous pink-and-white Shasta trailer. I surveyed the scene as my family helped me prepare for the upcoming festival. Tomorrow was the start of the four-day annual Summer Arts and Craft Fair in my hometown of Gatlinburg, Tennessee. Selling my art was my full-time job now, so I had to make the next few days a success.

The event was being held at the county fairgrounds. Nestled in the middle of a wooded area was an open space that was the perfect location for all kinds of events held year-round, such as the harvest festival in the fall, the Old Timey Christmas Festival, the Spring Tulip Festival, and many other events all summer.

My vendor spot was number forty-one. My adorable little travel trailer would be my home away from home now. I planned on spending a lot of time in it as I traveled the country, bringing my art to each and every state. It would be a fun adventure. At least that was what I reminded myself. I wouldn't be alone in the trailer. My furry companion, a perky white Chihuahua, was always by my side. One of his oversize ears flopped down, and that was how he'd gotten the name Van Gogh.

Currently, my family was on site helping me with my trailer. Mostly they wanted to snoop to see what this new endeavor was all about. My father ran a small engine repair shop right next to my parents' house. He was also a genius at fixing up classic cars—Corvettes, Camaros, GTOs. My mother had the full-time job of keeping my father and brothers out of trouble. Everyone said I looked a lot like my mother, with dark hair and big brown eyes the shade of a scrumptious piece of Godiva chocolate. My two brothers, Stevie and Hank, worked with my father in the shop. The three of them bickered all the time. Oddly, I knew that was their way of showing affection to one another.

Stevie and Hank had been "helping" me since my earliest memory. Like the time they helped repair my tricycle by taking it apart. Every single piece was set out on the front lawn like a jigsaw puzzle. They'd acted as if it was an innocent gesture of kindness. Or when I was in high school and they helped my date for the senior prom by taking him for a ride before the big night. My date was terrified to come anywhere near my house after that. They were my big brothers, though, and I loved them.

"We're going to make this the best-looking booth in the craft fair," my mother said with a wave of her hand.

My father mumbled under his breath as he tried to untangle the string lights that were meant to hang along the front of my trailer. My mother had volunteered my father for the job. It wasn't that he didn't want to help, it was just that he always had the best intentions but something disastrous happened.

"Look, the lights are tiny little campers just like yours." My mother pointed. "I ordered them from Amazon."

"They're great, Mom, but we'd better help Papa before he trips over the lights and kills himself."

I had the rest of the evening to set up for the craft fair. It had seemed like plenty of time at first, but now I was realizing the sun had set quite some time ago and the clock was ticking. I had to make sure I had all my paintings, blank canvases, and paint for when inspiration came, not to mention I needed to make sure I had everything planned for the setup. If customers couldn't see my paintings, they surely wouldn't buy them.

"I love that you got some of your art framed." My mother touched one of the gold frames.

"I thought it was nice to make some available already framed and some without, in case customers want to pick out their own frames."

"That's good thinking. Isn't our daughter smart?" My mother turned her attention back to my father.

My father mumbled something unintelligible again as he attempted to get the lights untangled from around his neck.

"I told you he'd hang himself." I ran over to him. "How did you do that, Papa?"

My mother and I spun my dad around so that the lights would come undone from around his neck.

"Can you breathe okay?" I fanned him.

He waved his hand. "I'm fine. Don't fuss."

My mother rolled her eyes. "He'd say he was fine even if he was blue-faced and passed out on the ground."

"Hey, is this thing supposed to be locked?" Stevie yelled out.

Just then, the back of the trailer tipped, making one side shoot up in the air like a seesaw.

"What have you done?" I shouted.

Hank ran over to help Stevie. "That's not how you do it. Let me show you how it's done."

As Hank raced toward the trailer like a bull charging toward the matador's red cape, he tripped over his own feet and landed face-first in the mud.

"Oh, for Pete's sake," my mother said.

Stevie laughed. "Thanks for the help, bro."

"Let me show you all how it's done." I gestured for everyone to step out of the way.

"Be careful, honey," my mother called out.

The guy who'd sold me the trailer had showed me all about it. Sure, I wasn't an expert, but I couldn't be any worse at this than my brothers.

As I worked on the hitch, my mother yelled at my father, "Be careful on that ladder."

Oh no. He had the ladder. This wouldn't end well. Would the rest of the evening be spent in the emergency room? Once I secured the hitch, I hurried over to my father's side. I held the ladder as he teetered on the edge of the top rung. The roll of tape slipped from his hands, landing on the ground. As soon as I let go of the ladder to pick up the tape, the ladder swayed and my father tumbled to the ground.

"I knew that would happen," my mother said.

While I helped my father to his feet, Van snatched the roll of tape and darted toward the nearby giant oak tree.

"Van, come back with the tape." I chased after my four-legged companion.

Of course, he thought this was a game and was determined to win. My brothers yelled for Van to stop as they ran behind me. After a couple of minutes of playing chase-the-Chihuahua around the old oak tree, I scooped up Van with the roll of tape still dangling from his mouth.

I handed the tape back to my father. "Are you okay, Papa?"

"I've had worse falls than that," he said.

Unfortunately, that was true.

"Do you think you should climb back on that ladder?" I asked as he walked away.

"There's no talking to him. He won't listen," my mother said.

We watched as my father climbed back onto the ladder with my brothers supervising. Stevie and Hank bickered back and forth about who would hold the ladder.

"I've never seen such chaos," a female voice said from over my shoulder.

I spun around to find my best friend, Sammie, standing behind me. Samantha Sutton, or Sammie as everyone affectionately called her, and I had been friends since first grade. Of course, to be friends for that long we had a lot in common. We both liked eighties music, lounging by the pool in the summer, and bargain shopping. As for appearance, we were complete opposites. Sammie was tall, with long legs, and I was short. She had blond hair cut into a bouncy bob and I had long, dark hair.

"When did you get here?" I asked as I reached out to hug her.

"You mean, how much of this scene did I witness? Enough to see that it's business as usual for the Cabots."

I blew the hair out of my eyes. "Welcome to my world."

"I'm fully aware of your world, remember? It's been this way for the total of all the years I've known you." She handed me a pretty pink package.

She knew how much I loved the color pink. Pretty much everyone knew pink was my signature color when they spotted my old pink truck pulling the pink trailer.

"What is this?"

"A little something I thought might make you feel better."

"You bought me a gift? Why did you do that? You didn't have to do that." I immediately untied the white ribbon.

"I know I didn't have to, but it's just that tomorrow is a big day for you. A whole new start to life." She moved her arm in a sweeping gesture. "It deserves a celebration."

I hugged her again. "Thank you. You're such a great friend."

"Hurry and open it. I want to see if you like it."

I hurriedly opened the package. The suspense was getting to me. My mother had slipped over to see what all the fuss was about.

"Oh, you're ruining the paper," my mother said. "We could reuse that."

My mother wanted to keep every bit of gift wrap she saw. We'd exchanged the same gift bags back and forth for six years now. If one got smashed or ripped she grieved for days.

I eased the pink paper away from the box and handed it to my mother. She slowly folded it, as if it were a piece of delicate silk. I pulled the mug from the box. A self-portrait of Vincent Van Gogh was on each side.

"Do you love it? When you pour in hot liquid his ear disappears."

I laughed. "It's perfect."

"Interesting," my mother said.

The sound of a motor caught our attention. The man in charge of organizing the craft fair was driving a golf cart down the path in front of our booths. With his wide shoulders and hefty stature, Evan Wright barely fit behind the wheel of the vehicle.

"Who's this guy?" Stevie asked with a hint of suspicion in his voice.

"He's the guy in charge here," I whispered.

"He seems shady if you ask me," Hank said.

My brothers, mother, and father were suspicious of everyone. I tried not to be that way, although I supposed on occasion I succumbed to that attitude too.

Evan rolled to a stop in front of my booth. "It's a bit late to be out, don't you think?"

"There's a curfew?" Sammie asked.

Evan eyed Sammie. "No curfew, but people are trying to sleep because they'll be up early in the morning. I heard a lot of ruckus over here."

"Ruckus," Hank said with a chortle. "That's a funny-sounding word."

Stevie laughed too.

My mother smacked them on the back of the head with the gift wrap remnants. She meant business if she was jeopardizing her paper.

Evan tapped his fingers against the steering wheel while waiting for an answer. The gold ring on his finger clanked against the metal of the wheel.

"We were just wrapping up," I said with a forced smile.

He scrutinized all of us for a bit longer before accelerating away.

"That was weird," Sammie said.

"Well, it takes all kinds," my mother said.

"Ta-da," Papa said.

The string lights glowed in the night sky. They added just the right amount of coziness to the area. It didn't feel quite as lonesome now. I'd worried that I'd get lonely once my family left. Yes, I couldn't believe I'd thought that, but I had.

I hugged my father. "The lights are fantastic. Thank you, Papa."

"Well, I should go and let you get some rest before your big day tomorrow." Sammie raised her voice, hoping my family would take the hint and leave too.

She'd obviously noticed my yawning. The family didn't catch subtle hints, or if they did, they ignored them. Tomorrow was Friday, the start of the fair. I needed to rest for the big event, but with my excitement, I wasn't sure how I'd ever fall asleep.

My mother surprisingly picked up the clue. "Boys, it's time to go." She clapped her hands.

Somehow my mother rounded up my brothers and father. Sammie left too. I clutched Van in my arms. It was just the two of us. Tomorrow was the big day.

CHAPTER 2

Travel trailer tip 2:
Home is where you park it.

"I want to return this horrible painting." The tall, willowy, gray-haired woman placed the framed canvas down on the table in front of me.

Earlier, when she'd purchased the art piece from me, she'd been impeccably dressed and practically flawless. Now, just a few hours later, she was a hot mess. Her hair tumbled around her flushed face and dark circles colored under her icy-blue eyes. Her white blouse and navy-blue trousers were now in desperate need of an iron, as if she'd slept in the clothing. Who was I to notice such things, though? My outfit had fared worse. I peered down at my paint-stained jeans. Various colors decorated the front of my white T-shirt too.

"Is there something wrong with the painting?" I asked.

She placed her hands on her slender hips. "Is there something wrong?" Now she was mocking me. "Yes, you could say that something is wrong."

Van Gogh yipped at the woman as he wiggled in my arms. He acted as if he wanted down so that he could chase her away. In reality, in the face of any danger he would run and hide in the trailer. She glared at him. He wouldn't bite her unless she tried to pet him. Or if she turned her back and I let him down. Van had been protective of me since the day I'd rescued him from the animal shelter.

Claiming she had changed her mind wouldn't be a good enough reason for a return in my opinion, but what else could be the problem? If she didn't want it, I would have to give her the money back. I was happy with my sales so far at the fair, but a return would be a financial setback.

"What seems to be the problem?" I used the sweetest tone possible.

I'd never forget the evening I painted the aforementioned piece of art. Rain had battered against the windows of my cottage, almost in rhythm with each stroke of my brush. Thunder rattled the walls and lightning had caused the lights to flicker on and off. The dense trees surrounding my place acted almost as a comforting, earthy embrace. While at home, I always felt safe from the overwhelming and hectic world.

Oil paint had been my preferred medium to bring the portrait to life. The subject of my work had popped into my mind as clear as any living person. It was as if she was pleading with me to immortalize her on the canvas. I had no idea who she was, but I knew her beauty had to be captured. She wore an ornately trimmed red-and-gold Victorian era gown with her dark hair pulled up into a French twist. That was exactly how I'd depicted her in the portrait.

"The painting is haunted," the woman said without batting an eyelash.

I surveyed my surroundings to see if anyone else was in on this joke. Fairgoers milled around the grounds with other artists selling their wares. No one was paying attention to me or my disgruntled customer.

"Did Evan put you up to this?" I asked around a laugh.

The lines between her stone-cold eyes deepened. "I don't know Evan. Frankly, I'm insulted that you would accuse me of anything that devious."

Uh-oh. Now I was riling her up even more. Apparently, she was completely serious. She was a few strokes short of a finished portrait.

"Why do you think the painting is haunted?" Curiosity made me ask this question.

"Right after I bought it, I took it home and hung it up. Immediately, strange things happened. Things that had never happened before, so I knew it had to be this painting causing the chaos." She gestured toward the canvas.

I frowned. "What type of strange things?"

She tossed up her hands in frustration. "Doors slamming, unexplained footsteps, and the painting was knocked off the wall and landed on the floor all the way across the room."

That sounded like something out of a scary movie. Still, I had my doubts that this woman was telling the truth. I didn't believe in ghosts.

Grabbing my bag, I pulled out the cash she had

given me less than four hours earlier. "Here you are. One hundred dollars."

It pained me to let go of the money. I had big plans for those crisp twenty-dollar bills—like buying food.

She counted the bills to make sure I hadn't stiffed her. What kind of operation did she think I was running? After all, she was the one who thought the painting was haunted. What a crazy idea. I pushed my shoulders back and held my head high. It would be all right. Another buyer would come along who appreciated my work.

I wanted to ask her more about this "haunting," but I thought better of it. Clearly, she was just making this up in order to return the painting. Plus, even if I changed my mind and decided to ask, it wasn't an option now. She turned and hurried away before another word was exchanged. At least that tête-à-tête was over, and now I could go back to work.

After placing the painting back on the easel next to the other canvases, I picked up my brush to add a little more detail to my current project. While I waited for other customers to come by, I painted. I'd done fairly well at this show so far, selling four paintings already. Since this was Friday, I had the rest of the weekend ahead of me and, with any luck, I'd sell even more. My fingers were crossed I wouldn't receive another return.

This time I was working on a portrait of a young woman and her horse. The inspiration had come from a woman I'd seen riding at a nearby farm. I thought it would make a lovely painting. Now I was creating it from memory.

For most of my paintings, I used oil paint. In my opinion, the oil made it easier to get just the right look. My interest with art had started at the age of fourteen. It was hard to believe that had been over ten years ago now. The only time I'd had any art training was a class in high school. That changed a few years ago, when I'd decided to take classes at night. Things had come up that prevented me from attending college—things like no money—but as the years slipped away, I'd decided it was now or never. I'd taken a job at my Aunt Patsy's diner and worked there up until two weeks ago. I figured six years was enough and it was time for a change.

"I'm quite impressed by your work." The female voice snapped my attention away from the colors in front of me.

The woman studied the canvas. Her hair color reminded me of the chocolate-brown paint color I used often. A rich brown with earthy gray undertones. She stared at the portrait the other woman had just returned. A potential new customer? Could I get that lucky? The woman was even shorter than me, at probably five foot. Her long, straight hair reached past her waist. In some ways she reminded me of my mother. They were probably close to the same age.

"Thank you," I said, putting down my brush.

Her comment was just the boost I had needed after the earlier encounter with the unhappy customer.

The woman studied the portrait through her thick black eyeglasses. "Did you add the skull in her dress on purpose?"

I frowned. "I'm sorry. What do you mean?"

She pointed. "On the woman's dress there's a skull. It's an interesting touch. Quite haunting."

I moved around the table and now stood beside her. The earthy scent of patchouli encircled her. Staring at the portrait, I still couldn't see the skull. Was she just as nutty as the other customer?

"You don't see it, do you?" she asked.

"No, I'm sorry."

She removed her eyeglasses and examined the portrait again. "That's odd. When I look at it without my glasses, it's not there."

"Maybe there's a reflection or smear on your glasses," I said.

After wiping them with the edge of her bohemian-style shirt, she placed them back on her face. "It's still there."

I wasn't quite sure what to say.

She removed the eyeglasses once again. "Here, you put them on and tell me what you see."

This was the second odd experience I'd had in less than an hour. My life had always been uneventful. Apparently, I was making up for that now. Nonetheless, I took the frames and put them on as she'd asked. Whoa, I'd get a headache quickly wearing them. Once my eyes adjusted, I peered at the portrait. It was exactly as she'd described.

"Do you see it?" she asked excitedly.

"I see it now. I never painted that. At least not on purpose."

"Maybe it was just a trick of the strokes," she said.

"I'm sure no other paintings would have this."

Keeping her eyeglasses on, I moved to the right

a couple of steps. Her Birkenstocks squeaked with her movement. Peering at another painting, I couldn't believe my eyes. Another image was in this painting. This time it was a skeleton, not just a skull. A shiver ran down my spine. I pulled the eye-glasses off.

"What do you see?" the woman asked.

The skeleton wasn't visible without the eye-glasses. I handed them back to her.

'It's a skeleton." My voice was barely above a whisper.

She put on the black-rimmed eyeglasses and stud-ied the painting. "Oh, I see it too. You didn't do that on purpose? That's amazing. You have such talent."

I shook my head no, still in shock. The woman stepped around me to examine the other artwork I had on display. "Oh, there's a hidden image in all of them."

I couldn't wrap my mind around how this had happened. If it had occurred only once, I would think it was a fluke, but that couldn't be the case when it occurred in all of them. Was it just her eye-glasses? Yes, that had to be the case. This was an-other joke. The woman claiming the painting was haunted was a joke, and now someone was playing another trick on me. I wanted to identify the prankster.

"Who put you up to this?" I asked.

She furrowed her brow. "I don't know what you're implying, but I'm not fooling around. I have the booth two down from you. I make jew-elry."

I peered down the lane at her table, full of jew-elry on display. It was hard to see from this distance, but her jewelry seemed as if it was made with various stones.

She caught me studying her pieces and said, "I use sliced gemstones like agate, jasper, onyx, and more."

"Sounds lovely. Back to the painting, though. I'm sorry, but it has to be your eyeglasses," I said.

"Do you have anything else glass?" she asked.

"I have a jar I use to clean my brushes." I gestured toward the picnic table where it sat.

"I wonder if you could see the image through that too? Or if it has to be magnified?"

I rushed over and retrieved the jar. Lifting it up to my face, I peered through the glass at the painting. A gasp escaped my mouth when I spotted the skull.

"See. I told you it wasn't my eyeglasses. You should be happy. This is a true talent and a work of art. Embrace it." She patted me on the back.

Moving from painting to painting, I examined each one. They all featured some kind of hidden image. I suppose I had to believe it now because I was seeing it with my own eyes. How did this happen? I hadn't planned it. I suppose I had painted the images with my subconscious.

"My name's Ruth Gordon, by the way." She stretched out her hand toward me.

I shook her hand. "Celeste Cabot. Nice to meet you."

"Are you okay? I still can't believe you didn't know about this."

"No idea," I said, still eyeing the painting.

The more I looked at the woman in the portrait, the more I noticed her eyes. They seemed different now somehow, but I couldn't put my finger on why I thought that. The hum of the motor cart returned. Evan cruised down the path toward us.

"Good morning, ladies. I guess you're not having any luck with selling your wares, if you have time to hang around and chitchat." His loud, boisterous laugh carried across the summer air.

Evan didn't wait for an answer. He punched the pedal, jerking his head backward. His laughter continued as he drove off.

"I don't like that guy," Ruth said with disdain in her voice.

"He's not pleasant, is he?" I asked.

"I've overheard quite a few vendors talking about how much they don't like him. As a matter of fact, I might not come back next year if he's still here."

"I certainly understand why you feel that way," I said. "Like my grandma always says, he's as useful as a pogo stick in quicksand."

"Oh, it looks as if I have customers. It was nice meeting you, Celeste." She tossed her hand up in a wave and rushed away to help her customers.

Now I was alone, staring at the woman's portrait. Or was she staring at me?

CHAPTER 3

Travel trailer tip 3:
Explore your campgrounds. Make note of areas
of interest—such as the ice cream vendor.

Late in the afternoon, things slowed down at the craft fair. Ruth agreed to watch over my booth while I took a stroll around the grounds to check out the other vendors' wares. I'd do the same for her. Rumor had it that a lot of artists working with acrylics would be at the fair. That meant stiff competition for me. How would I compare? I had no idea if my prices were competitive or if my work would be half as good as theirs.

I carried Van in my arms, although I had his leash in case he wanted to walk. His tiny legs got tired easily. I totally understood. At five foot two, my stride wasn't big either, and I never got anywhere quickly.

Right away, I passed three vendors whose paintings were stunning. Thank goodness I felt my prices were in line with theirs. I questioned whether my work was good enough, but my mother always reminded me that I was my own worst critic.

I stopped at a vendor who made leather items. Things like belts, bracelets, and key chains. A caged leather bracelet with tiny faux pearls caught my attention. The artist eyed me first and turned her focus to Van. Spikes of strawberry blond hair topped her head. She wore a white tank top and light beige linen pants to no doubt help fight the heat.

"He doesn't bite . . . unless you try to pet him," I said with a smirk.

She raised a thin eyebrow. "Oh . . . well, he's cute."

"Thank you." I picked up the bracelet.

Van barked. I couldn't tell if he was thanking her for the compliment or it was a warning for her not to come close.

"Your work is lovely," I said, moving on to a stamped key chain.

"Thank you." She set down the punching tool she'd been holding. "I've seen you around. You have a booth here too, right?"

"Yes. Just down the way by the big oak tree." I gestured.

She crossed her arms in front of her chest. "So what do you think of the craft fair so far?"

"It's good, but because it's my first one, I have nothing to compare it to yet," I said.

"Business is a bit slow, but that doesn't surprise me really." She blew the bangs out of her eyes. "I'll be lucky if I sell anything. And I really need the money right now."

Van wiggled, so I let him walk around on his leash.

"Oh really?" I asked.

"I think it's because of that Evan Wright. He doesn't know what he's doing. Plus, his personality is so off-putting, it doesn't surprise me that people stay away."

"Yes, he is a bit rough around the edges."

"A bit?" She narrowed her apple-green-colored eyes. "I'd like to tell him what's on my mind. He comes by here all the time, criticizing me and my work."

"That's not nice of him," I said.

"No, it isn't. If he keeps testing my patience, I'll tell him too." She picked up one of the sharp tools beside her and stabbed a strip of leather.

My heart skipped a beat. Van barked. She seemed extremely upset.

"Maybe if I had a talk with him . . ."

"Feel free, but I doubt it will do any good." She cut a piece of leather, dismissing my suggestion.

Maybe if I changed the subject, it would make her feel better.

"How do you make such lovely items?" I asked. Honestly, I wasn't just asking in an attempt to make feel better. I was genuinely interested.

She eyed me up and down as if she was suspicious. After a couple of seconds she picked up a leather cuff bracelet and said, "Well, like with this one, I use strap pieces of leather to make each bracelet unique. I stamp the design on the leather and secure the beads around the edges. The stamps are used with ink to dye the leather. I made the pattern for the bird design with my computer."

If I had the extra cash, I would have totally bought the bracelet. Maybe if she still had it at the end of the fair, I could splurge.

"Your work is great," I said.

"Thank you," she said in a slightly less harsh tone this time.

"Well, good luck with selling your items," I said. "My name's Celeste Cabot, by the way."

"Carly Koy," she said. "Nice to meet you."

"If you need anything, feel free to come down and get me." I gestured down the path toward my trailer.

"That's nice of you, thank you."

I waved and headed down the way a bit more. I made eye contact with another woman. A ginger-colored mane peeked out from under her royal-blue baseball cap advertising a local restaurant called Bob's Burgers. Her green eyes matched the needles on the nearby pine tree.

I stopped to take a look at her jewelry. Vast arrays of colors decorated the two tables full of beaded necklaces, bracelets, and earrings. Everything from turquoise, onyx, and pearl to cooper. I liked the way she knotted the beads together on the necklaces to make a waterfall effect.

"How's business?" she asked.

"Oh, you saw me at my booth?" I asked with a smile.

"After a bit you start to recognize faces," she said.

"It's not bad, I suppose."

Other than someone returning a haunted painting. Unfortunately, I couldn't share that because she would think I was bonkers. Van squirmed in my arms, so I let him down. He walked around sniffing things on the ground while I held his leash.

"I'm Celeste Cabot," I said.

"Shar Pricket," she said, sticking her hand out toward me.

Van didn't protest her getting too close to me because he was busy checking out a cricket. The insect hopped away and he barked in its wake.

Movement caught my attention. Someone was approaching Shar's booth. The sun was setting and casting a shadow across the man's face. Finally, when he neared, I realized it was Evan. Shar saw me watching someone, so she turned to see who was approaching the booth. A groan slipped from her lips.

"What does he want?" she whispered.

It looked as if we were about to find out.

"Hello, ladies, how are things?" Evan wiggled his thick, bushy eyebrows.

"Fine," Shar said through gritted teeth.

"You need to move the tables back two inches." He tapped the edge of the nearby display table.

She eyed him.

He waved his hand in front of her face. "Hello? Anyone home?" He turned his attention to me. "Look, she's a zombie."

Loud, boisterous laughter spilled from his mouth. I stared at him in shock too.

He frowned. "I'll let it go tonight, but I expect you'll correct it by tomorrow."

The sun shone off the ring on Evan's finger. He wore the same one I'd noticed on the first night. In the daylight I had more time to examine it. The sparkle was almost blinding. It had a single diamond on each side of the ring and smaller diamonds on top. A scroll pattern in black wrapped around the diamonds on the top. The ring was unusual and captured my attention right away.

He caught me looking at the ring. "I had it designed. It was all my idea." His voice boomed with pride.

"It's lovely," I said.

He narrowed his eyes at me, as if maybe I was trying to take the ring from him. I only said it was lovely, not that I wanted it. He was so strange. I honestly didn't know what to make of his behavior. I didn't wear much jewelry anyway. A small diamond and pearl ring my parents had given me for my twenty-first birthday were all I wore. Maybe a locket necklace or some pearls for special occasions. I liked to keep things simple and basic, like T-shirts, jeans, and tennis shoes. That was my style.

He walked away.

Shar turned to face me. "Can you believe that guy? Two inches? My tables have been in the same spot since I arrived. He's just looking for stuff to harass me over. Does he have nothing better to do?"

When Van shivered, I picked him up and cuddled him in my arms. "It does seem as if he's nit-picking."

Shar focused her dark-circle-lined eyes on me. She seemed extra small against the backdrop of her large, shiny, chrome camper.

"If he messes with me, I'll knock him into the middle of next week looking both ways for Sunday." Shar pumped her fist.

Obviously, Evan made her extremely mad. Though I thought surely she was only joking about knocking him into next Sunday. Shar seemed too nice to actually punch Evan.

"If you need help moving your tables, let me know," I said.

She scoffed. "I'm not moving the tables. If he doesn't like it, let him move them. And he'd better not damage any of my items in the process."

Oh no; it looked as if a confrontation might take place tomorrow. I should avoid the area with Van.

"Well, it was nice meeting you. I need to get back; it's getting dark."

"Nice meeting you too," she said.

I knew by her tone that she was still angry with Evan. I didn't like him either, but I certainly wasn't going to let him get under my skin. I headed down the path toward my booth. Van was looking around as I carried him in my arms.

"Van, are you hungry?" I asked, scratching behind his ears.

Ruth was standing behind the two booths when I returned. "I figured I could watch both this way."

I laughed. "That's a good idea."

"Well, I'm going to pack up my things for the evening."

"Me too," I said.

After placing Van in the trailer, I filled his dish with food and put more water into the other one. He loved getting cozy in his little bed. I collapsed onto the bed for a moment's rest. Not too long, though. There was too much work to do.

My pink-and-white retro trailer was awesome, but space was limited. I'd brought only the essentials. My supplies were crammed into a corner. Paints, canvases, and an easel. The benches and table tucked into the back of the trailer converted into a bed. My grandmother had made me a pink-and-white quilt for the bed. I'd added several toss pillows. One had pink hearts and the others were pink gingham.

My brothers had installed a metal-hitched storage area to the back of my trailer. They'd even painted it the exact shade of pink so it matched. Now I had room to haul more of my paintings. I gathered up the paintings and placed them in the storage area of the trailer. I secured the lock and picked up a few pieces of trash that had found their way in front of my area.

Time had slipped away as I drifted off. I hadn't meant to nap. I suppose I'd been exhausted from the undertaking of a full day of craft fair duties. Night had come and darkness had taken over. The string lights my father had installed along the outside of my trailer lit up the small area around me. I'd just tossed the trash into the garbage can when shouting caught my attention. I stopped and peered down the path to see what was happening. It was hard to make out, but several people had gathered in front of what looked like Carly Koy's booth. I hoped she was all right.

Ruth appeared from around the side of her shiny-new, white-and-black Hummingbird travel trailer. I bet that thing had all kinds of fancy features. Nevertheless, I loved my pink beauty.

Ruth seemed less put together this time. Her black Grateful Dead band T-shirt was wrinkled, along with her long, gauzy white skirt.

"What's going on?" Ruth's question held a splash of annoyance.

"I don't know. We should go check it out," I said.

Ruth and I hurried down the path. When we arrived in front of Carly's booth, other vendors had gathered as well. Carly appeared distraught as she waved her arms while talking with Shar.

I stepped over to Carly and asked, "What happened?"

"Someone took my money. All the money I've made since I've been at the fair." The pain was evident in her voice.

"I'm sorry, Carly. When did this happen?"

She shook her head. "It was there a short time ago. Right after I spoke with you, I counted my cash. I put away my things. After that I went back to make sure I'd counted it correctly and the money was gone."

"Did someone call the police?" I asked.

"They're on their way." She pushed a strand of her strawberry blond hair away from her face.

Right away, I noticed the scarlet-colored drops on the back of her hand.

"Did you hurt your hand?" I asked.

Carly looked down and shoved her hands into her pockets. "I'm fine."

"Did you see anyone suspicious around?" Ruth asked.

"The only person I saw was Evan. He was here talking with Celeste and me earlier."

Now I was worried about my money. Who would do something like this? Surely not another vendor. They knew how hard it was to make and sell their items.

I spotted blue flashing lights from a police car.

It pulled up nearby and parked. A uniformed officer got out of the cruiser and walked over to where we stood. I peered up at his tall frame. Just a hint of dark hair peeked out from under his cap. The blue shirt and pants were precisely pressed, as if he'd just picked them up from the cleaners.

"What seems to be the problem?" he asked.

"Someone took my money." Carly waved her arms. "It's all gone. Whoever did this is going to pay."

"All right, calm down. Step over here and tell me what happened," the young officer said.

Ruth and I stepped away so the officer could speak with Carly. We headed down the path toward our trailers. The silvery moonlight illuminated the lane guiding us in the right direction. The scent of honeysuckle drifted across the night breeze.

"Who do you think did this?" I asked.

"I think maybe she just misplaced the money. It'll probably turn up soon." Ruth's bangle bracelets jingled as she gestured.

"I certainly hope so," I said. "We should take precautions so we don't find ourselves in the same predicament."

"Do you keep money in your trailer?" Ruth asked.

I studied her face. "Until I can take it to the bank. I probably won't now."

"Oh, I wouldn't worry about it. No need to take your money to the bank. Just put it in a safe place. You do put it in a safe place, right?" Ruth raised an eyebrow.

"Yes," I said.

I wouldn't offer more of an answer than that. Where I kept my money was my secret. What if the thief overheard me say where I kept my cash? No need to put myself at even more of a risk.

It had been a tiring day. The sun had set a couple of hours before, and I was ready for rest. I'd thought about enjoying the beautiful night sky, but now I wasn't sure if I wanted to hang around outside alone. The pitch-black sky showcased a million sparkling stars. The familiar feeling stirred inside me. The voice whispered in my ear that I should paint a scene just like the one around me.

When I reached my trailer, I turned around to survey the scene. Down the path, I saw that people had dispersed from the front of Carly's booth and the police had gone too. I hoped Carly found her money. I needed to make sure I kept my cash secure. I didn't have a large sum, but what I had was mine and I didn't want anyone to take it. I had worked hard for that money.

"Well, I'll see you in the morning." Ruth waved as she walked toward her trailer.

She seemed nice, but something about her also seemed a bit off. When she smiled, it didn't seem genuine. I suppose I had inherited my grandmother's skepticism. She believed people never displayed their true selves. It was always an act, she said. That wasn't to say people weren't nice, but she warned of being cautious even when you thought you knew someone well.

Now I was all alone in front of my tiny trailer. The faint sound of chatter carried across the night air, but everyone around me had retired for the evening. I should do the same, but even though I was tired, I was still full of anxious energy.

Though the tiny voice in my head had told me to paint the stunning night scene, I needed to work on my current project. Now that the excitement had died down, I'd have a little dinner and work on my painting. That always helped me relax. The tiny refrigerator in my trailer didn't hold much. The next few days I predicted I'd eat a lot of peanut butter and jelly sandwiches. After adding a glob of spread and grape jelly to the bread, I carried my sandwich out to the bench, enjoying my sandwich in the comfort of my cozy trailer.

CHAPTER 4

Travel trailer tip 4:
Know your exact camping location in case you need
emergency help. You can't just say "near the big tree."

As I sat in my trailer, I dined on a peanut butter and grape jelly sandwich. For dessert, I'd have a banana. It was hard having a gourmet meal while living in a small space. Not that I wanted that anyway. The simpler things in life were what I enjoyed most. My dinners consisted of paper plates and plastic utensils. At least I had electricity and plumbing. As much as I loved the trailer, I was always glad to go home to my quaint cottage house. I lived in a house on the edge of my parents' property. Sometimes I wondered if it was a bit too close.

Van sat at my feet, waiting for me to drop a crumb. After I finished eating, he made one last, sniffing loop around the floor in case he'd missed a morsel before giving up and curling up in his comfy, paw-print bed. The lining I'd added had been made by my grandmother. She'd quilted it to match mine in the same pattern, with blue and white patches of fabric.

The longer I sat there, the more anxious I became. In my opinion, Evan should hire a security guard for the fair. He probably wouldn't go for that, though. It wouldn't hurt to ask though, right?

I grabbed my keys and headed for the door. "Van, I'll be right back."

He opened one eye and looked at me but went back to his nap. I hurried out the door, locked it, and headed down the path toward Evan's trailer. He was staying at the fair like most everyone else. From his constant scowl and grumpy disposition, it didn't seem as if he liked his job much.

A gentle breeze carried across the warm night air. Crickets chirped in the nearby trees. Fireflies lit up the dark of night. I wasn't sure why I thought speaking with Evan might be a good idea. He could be so rude. No doubt he would treat my request with utter disdain. As a fair vendor, I figured we had the right to feel somewhat safe while we were here, though.

I passed by Carly's trailer but saw no sign of her. The lights were off. I wondered if she'd found the money yet. Even if there was no one taking money, it was still a good idea to have security. Especially if she had really been robbed.

Next, I passed Shar's booth. The lights were out there too. I was surprised everyone went to bed so early. I thought back to what she'd said about Evan. Still, I had to assume she had only been joking.

Soon, I reached his expansive, shiny, silver travel trailer. This thing even had a queen-size bed. I knew because my second cousin twice removed on my mom's side had a travel trailer like this one. If I had this thing, I'd feel like I was staying in a five-star hotel. I'd heard it wasn't Evan's but had been provided for his use by the organizers of the craft fair.

Because no lights were on inside, it was a bad sign that I would be able to speak with him tonight. I suppose I shouldn't knock on his door if he was sleeping. That would be like waking a hibernating bear. I would just have to talk with him tomorrow.

As I turned around to head back to my trailer, I spotted something out of the corner of my eye. I peered to my left for a better view. It looked as if someone was lying on the ground next to the trailer. Was it Evan? Was he hurt? I raced over to the motionless person. I was shocked to see Evan lying there.

"Evan, are you okay?" I called out.

He didn't answer. He didn't move at all. Was he alive? Panic surged through me as I decided what to do. Should I check to see if he was breathing? I leaned down to Evan. As I reached out to check his pulse, my hand shook. I moved my fingers toward him but stopped when I spotted what looked like a knife protruding from his neck.

The knife was short, with a wooden handle. I'd seen one like this before. Maybe I was wrong, but it looked as if something used for carving wood. Based on the position of the weapon, I'd say there was no way he could have done this to himself. Of course, I was no detective.

I pressed my fingertips to his neck. Nothing. I

had to call 911. Unfortunately, I'd left my phone at
my trailer. It would do no good to perform CPR.
How long had he been here? When was the last
time I'd seen him alive? It was at Carly's booth.
That had been right around sunset. This must
have happened shortly after.

I jumped up and raced around the corner of his
trailer. I hoped that I'd spot someone so I could
tell them to dial 911. It would be much faster than
going all the way back to my trailer. Someone had
killed Evan. That sent a shiver down my spine. A
murderer at the craft fair? The thought was terrify-
ing.

I'd just made it around the corner when I
smacked right into someone. The tall, muscular man
grabbed me and I screamed.

"Whoa, are you all right?" He looked into my
eyes.

It took me a second to form a sentence.

"Over there. The man is dead. He's been
stabbed." I pointed toward the side of the trailer.

The man frowned. "Where?"

He took off toward the side of the trailer before
I had a chance to answer. I followed behind him. I
had forgotten to tell him to call for help. Perhaps
he had a phone on him. When I reached the edge
of the trailer, I stopped. The man was next to
Evan.

With the faint light from the trailer, I got a better
view of this man. He had short, caramel-colored
hair with streaks of lighter blond, as if he'd been
out in the summer sun. Though his hair was a bit
tousled at the moment. He wore a white T-shirt

and navy-blue shorts. I noticed his shirt was on inside out, as if he'd dressed in a hurry.

He turned to look at me. "Have you called the police?"

I shook my head. "I don't have my phone on me."

He stood and pulled a phone from his pocket. I tried not to look down at the body while I listened to the man's side of the 911 call.

When he finished, he said, "They're on their way."

"That's a relief." I rubbed my arms to fight away the goose bumps. "Thank you for calling."

"Step over here with me," he said, guiding me toward the front of the trailer. "Did you find him?"

"Yes, I came by to speak with him. Ironically, I wanted to talk with him about security. Who could have done this to him?" I asked.

The man looked around. "Did you see anyone by Evan's trailer?"

"No, thank goodness," I said breathlessly.

"My name's Caleb Ward."

"Celeste Cabot. Do you have a booth here at the fair?"

"Yes, it's on the far side over there." He pointed across the way. "I do wood sculpting."

"Painter." I gestured with my thumb toward my chest.

Where were the police? I hated standing out here trying to act calm when Evan was over there with a knife in his neck. I felt as if I might hyperventilate.

A few seconds later, sirens sounded. The flashing lights appeared in the nearby parking area.

"We should go over there and direct the police to the trailer," Caleb said.

"That's a good idea," I said.

We headed toward the parking area. People were starting to come out of their trailers now. When I glanced to my right, I spotted Carly standing by one of the tall oak trees. She was watching us. After jumping out of their cruisers, the police rushed toward us.

"The body is over there by that trailer." Caleb pointed.

"Stay here," one of the officers instructed us.

He didn't have to tell me twice. Caleb and I stood there as several officers walked by toward the trailer. I supposed they would want me to tell them everything I'd seen. There really wasn't much to tell. I'd gone there and found Evan. The part about the knife in his neck they'd see for themselves.

"Are you all right?" Caleb asked, snapping me out of my thoughts.

"Yes, I'm fine. I need to get back to my trailer to check on my dog." I blew the hair out of my eyes.

"What kind of dog?" he asked.

Maybe he was just trying to distract me so I wouldn't stress, but I was finding it hard to make small talk right now.

"He's a Chihuahua," I said.

"I have a German shepherd," he said.

"My brother has a German shepherd," I said, still somewhat distracted.

The lights from the police cars cast a blue glow over the area. I looked over toward the oak tree where I'd seen Carly. She was no longer there. I scanned the crowd for her but didn't see her any-where. A tall man wearing a suit walked by. He seemed out of place with that clothing. I assumed he must be the homicide detective. He spoke with a few of the officers. One of them pointed in our direction.

"It looks as if they are talking about us now," Caleb said.

My anxiety increased as the man in the tan suit headed over to us. Maybe now I could speak with him and get back to my trailer. I just wanted to put distance between myself and the crime scene. Finding Evan had been disconcerting, to say the least.

"Are you the person who called 911?" the raven-haired man in the suit asked.

"She found the body." Caleb pointed at me.

Oh, great. Way to rat me out. I held my hand up in acknowledgment because it seemed my voice had become nothing more than a barely audible squeak. If I seemed too nervous, would they think I had something to do with Evan's murder?

The man pulled out his notepad and pen. "I'm Detective Pierce Meyer with the Gatlinburg Police Department. What's your name?"

"Celeste Cabot." I managed.

"You're a vendor here at the craft fair?"

Now was certainly not the time to notice this man's dreamy eyes. The artist in me couldn't help myself, though. The nearby trailers had all switched on lights, which allowed me a better look at the cop-per and green colors in his eyes. The playful, up-ward tilt of his full lips didn't go unnoticed by me either.

"Yes, that's right," I said.

How had he known? I suppose all the customers had gone. Plus, I had paint all over my clothing. That was a good indication that some crafting had taken place in my past. He jotted down my name and turned his attention to Caleb. He gave the detective his name.

"Did either of you touch the body?" he asked.

I raised my hand as if this was a pop quiz. "Only to check for a pulse."

"Do you have any idea who may have wanted to harm the victim?" Detective Meyer asked.

For a split second I thought about answering "everyone at the craft fair." But surely there was no one here who disliked Evan enough to actually murder him.

So instead, I said, "Not that I'm aware of."

The detective looked at Caleb. "How about you, sir? Do you know of anyone?"

"No, I can't imagine. I didn't really know the guy," Caleb said.

"Why were you coming around the trailer at this time of night?" the detective looked at me and asked.

Did he think I had done this? Now I was really starting to worry. If I was in jail, who would take care of Van?

"I was coming to speak with Evan," I said.

"About what?" the detective asked.

"About adding security to the craft fair."

"Well, now we're talking . . ." The detective's voice rose. "What made you think you needed security?"

"Earlier this evening, one of the vendors had her money stolen," I said.

"Really? What's her name?"

"Carly Koy. That's spelled K-o-y. I saw it on the business cards she has on her booth table."

"Thanks for paying attention to the details." He jotted down the information. "All right. And you say she has a booth here?"

"Yes, it's the fourth one down right there with that turquoise trailer."

"I'll have a talk with her. Thank you."

"You're welcome," I said. "I'm surprised you hadn't heard about this yet."

He eyed me up and down with his sexy eyes. "I just came on shift. I'm sure I'll be briefed about everything soon."

"Right," I said, feeling slightly embarrassed.

"If you think of anything else, please let me know right away."

"Absolutely, I will," I said. "Is it all right if we leave? I have a dog waiting for me and he does too."

The detective looked from me to Caleb. "Sure, that's fine, but I'll be in touch."

Would the fair continue now that there had been a murder?

"I think it's best if I get out of here for good." I rubbed my arms as if fighting off a chill. I wanted nothing more than to get Van, jump into my pink pickup truck, and drive home to the safety of my little cottage.

Apparently, Detective Meyer had other plans. "I'm sorry, but we want everyone to remain here until we're finished with questioning."

"How long will that be?" I asked.

"We'll try to make it as quick as possible," Detective Meyer said.

That hadn't exactly answered my question.

"Thanks," I said half-heartedly.

Detective Meyer studied my face. "Rest assured, we'll find out who did this."

I never dreamed this night would end with me speaking with the Gatlinburg Police Department. Detective Pierce Meyer was a tall glass of water, but no matter how long he studied me with his penetrating hazel eyes, I wouldn't confess to something I didn't do.

I turned and headed toward the trailer. Caleb fell into step beside me.

"Don't be scared tonight, okay? I'm sure someone was targeting Evan," Caleb said. "I'm sure no one would ever hurt you."

I stopped and looked at Caleb. "How do you know that?"

"Well, I don't know for sure, but it's just that, you know, he was Evan. His personality probably made him have a few enemies," Caleb said.

"You think so?" I asked.

"Absolutely. You know Evan."

"Yeah, I had some dealings with him."

"And you're just so sweet. Like I said, no killer would want to do anything to you."

I scoffed. "I don't think a killer would care if someone was nice or not. They just have it in their heads to the eliminate people sometimes."

"But not all the time," he said.

I'd had enough of this conversation. "Thanks

again and I'll see you around," I said with a wave of my hand.

"See you around," Caleb said.

I hurried my steps so that I could get to my Shasta as quickly as possible. Not a single light shone from Ruth's trailer. I suppose she had no idea that anything had even happened. Well, that was probably for the best. She'd hear all about it in the morning.

The thought had barely left my mind when movement caught my attention and I spotted Ruth. She'd walked from around the side of her trailer. With her head down, she hadn't even noticed me.

"Ruth," I called out.

She jumped as she turned her attention my way. Her hair seemed unkempt, her clothing askew.

"Oh, I'm sorry if I startled you. Is everything okay?" I asked.

Maybe she had seen all the activity and gone to check it out.

"Everything's just fine," she said as she continued toward her trailer door.

I wanted to stop her to ask if she'd heard what had happened. She was in such a hurry, though, it didn't seem as if she wanted to talk right then. Her behavior was a bit odd, but I figured she was just tired and not in the mood for more chitchat.

With shaky hands, I opened the door to my trailer and stepped inside. Van looked up at me from his bed but didn't make an attempt to run over to greet me. He closed his eyes and went back to sleep.

"Thanks for the warm welcome home," I said around a laugh.

Obviously, he hadn't been too worried about me being gone a few minutes longer than I'd hoped.

The returned painting was still propped up against the wall where I'd left it. No matter where I moved it, her eyes seemed to follow me. I suppose it was just my imagination. There was no way the painting was haunted. It was impossible.

I hoped I would be able to sleep that night after what had happened. The benches that converted into a bed wasn't the most comfortable I'd ever slept on, but nevertheless, it was better than camping outside with the bugs and a possible killer.

CHAPTER 5

Travel trailer tip 5:
What happens in a travel trailer stays in a
travel trailer.

Tossing and turning in bed in the cramped space, I tried to sleep with my face pressed near the back of the bench. I fluffed my pillow and kicked off the quilt. Nothing worked. Van gave me the look before hopping off my bed and retreating to his own. The one that let me know I was disturbing his sleep.

"Sorry, pookie, but Mama can't sleep."

I closed my eyes and counted sheep. When I reached two hundred, I gave up. I was sure all the crazy events of the day were keeping me awake. I'd had a lot to take on in one day. Hauntings, strange artwork, a theft, and a murder. I hoped tomorrow would be less eventful. Evan had been hateful to a lot of people, but I felt terrible about what had happened to him. I couldn't get it out of my head that the killer could still be around the grounds right now, looking for the next victim.

As I lay there with my eyes closed, I couldn't shake the sensation that someone was watching me. I opened my eyes and looked at Van. He was completely engrossed in something. The white glow in the corner on the other side of the trailer by my easel lit up my little space.

When I looked to the left, I spotted her. I gasped and sat up in bed. Van jumped back onto my bed and scrambled close to me. I held him tight to my chest with one hand and pulled the covers closer to us with the other. As if the covers would act as a shield from this woman.

I couldn't believe my eyes. It was the woman from my painting. Only she wasn't in the painting. She was standing there like any other person. The longer I looked at her, the more solid she became. The white glow diminished, but the woman went nowhere. She watched me and I couldn't take my eyes off her. Had I lost my mind? Was this what the customer had told me about? How was this possible? I was completely freaked out. Should I speak to her?

"Hello?" I managed to mumble.

She offered no response. Her silence made me question my sanity. Though I suppose I would question my sanity more if she had spoken. Either way, panic raced through me. Van trembled as he watched the woman. She was scaring my dog. Therefore, she had to go.

No sooner had the thought entered my mind when the white glow returned. Little by little she faded, until I saw right through her. After a few more seconds, the glow was gone and so was she. The painting was still there, though, in the cramped spot kitty-corner to the door. The woman focused on me with her haunting dark eyes.

Van and I exchanged a look.

"What just happened?" I whispered.

No way could I fall asleep with the woman in the painting staring at me all night. I eased up from the bed as if she would pop out from the painting and grab me. I reached for the extra throw blanket I kept in a basket by the door. Trying not to get too close, I tossed the throw and hoped it landed over the painting.

Unfortunately, it landed on the floor. Her stare remained focused on me. Now I had to go over, pick up the blanket, and get it over the painting. I released a deep breath as I inched toward the painting. I didn't take my eyes off the woman's face. She still watched me. It was just a trick. Though I hadn't created the painting that way. The shadowing and light in the paint hadn't been right for that, but somehow now it was happening.

Van barked as I reached down for the blanket. I suppose he was telling me to be careful. My hands shook as I clutched the blanket and draped it over the painting. I moved as if I was feeding an alligator and trying not to get my hand bitten off. Once away from the painting, I released a deep breath.

"Well, that's a little better, right?"

Van jumped down from the bed and trotted to the other side of the trailer to get as far away as possible.

"Yeah, it's not much better, is it?"

Nonetheless, I had to get at least some sleep. I had paintings to finish. Plus, with any luck, I'd have a busy day tomorrow selling my art. I inched back over to the bed and jumped under the covers. Van raced over to me. I lifted the covers and he climbed under, snuggling up beside me. At least we had each other for protection. Chihuahuas might be small, but they always want to protect the people they love.

I suppose exhaustion finally took over because I drifted off to sleep. The sun shimmering through the openings of the blinds woke me. Strange things had taken place last night in my tiny trailer.

The blanket was still draped over the painting. I told myself it had to be a dream, but unless I'd been sleepwalking, it hadn't been. If I removed the blanket, would it still seem as if she was following me with her eyes? I wasn't sure I was ready to find out.

The sound of voices carried from what seemed to be right outside my trailer. I'd just gotten dressed in the khaki shorts I'd bought two seasons ago and the olive-green tank top my mother thought was in my color wheel. Shimmying into my clothing in a cramped space required a balancing act along with squeezing myself into the trailer's small bathroom. For breakfast I'd eaten a blueberry bagel. After picking up Van, I eased the door open. Ruth was standing outside near her trailer, talking with a tall, dark-haired man. They must have felt me watching them because they looked over. Ruth waved for me to join them.

"Good morning," I said as I stepped over.

Van trembled and tried not to look at them directly. He figured if he ignored them, they'd go away. I wished it worked that way. There were plenty of people I had ignored, who had never gone away.

"Celeste, I'd like for you to meet Max Stone. He'll be in charge of the fair from here on out." Ruth gestured toward the man. "It's tough, but he's working with the town council on the details from here on out."

"Nice to meet you." I stuck out my hand.

He didn't offer his hand in return. Instead, he glared at Van.

"Same to you," Max said.

Movement caught my attention. Down the path, several police officers walked around. The police were back.

"I thought they finished up last night." I motioned.

Max and Ruth looked over their shoulders. Oddly, they seemed similar in a strange way. I couldn't quite put my finger on why. Perhaps they had the same small, beady-shaped eyes, or the same downward slope to the corners of their mouths that made them appear to always be frowning. From the crinkles along her eyes and mouth, I figured Ruth was about twenty years older than Max.

"They just need to search again now that it's daylight," Max said.

Did Max worry that the killer would come after him? Could the murderer hold a grudge against whoever was in charge of the craft fair?

"It's terrible what happened. I didn't find out about it until this morning," Ruth said, looking down at her once-white, muddy tennis shoes.

"That must have been startling," I said.

"It was better than discovering the body." Ruth shivered at the thought.

I had been trying to forget, but that was next to impossible.

"Well, ladies, don't worry about anything because I have everything under control." Max puffed out his chest, apparently trying to look important, but only succeeding in looking like a bantam rooster.

"Will you be adding security now? I don't think I feel safe staying here without it." I studied his face.

"Yes, there will be a security guard." He checked the time on his gold wristwatch. "Any other questions?"

I shook my head. Why did he have such a snippy tone?

"I'll see you all around." Max turned to walk away.

"I didn't think it was possible, but he's just as annoying as Evan," I said.

"He seems nice enough. From what I understand, he's been helping Evan, so I guess they got along well," Ruth said. "I suppose I should get my stuff set out before people arrive."

She thought he seemed nice, but she hadn't liked Evan? They had the same personality, in my opinion.

"I'll see you later," I said.

Ruth waved as she headed back to her trailer. I put Van back in my trailer so that he could chew his bone while I set out the paintings. Should I place the haunted one in the trailer out there? Of course I should, right? Maybe someone would buy it. But could I knowingly sell a haunted painting? What was I thinking? Was I going bonkers? The painting couldn't truly be haunted. Though I knew what I'd seen.

Concentrating on painting was hard with the movement around the fair. It wasn't customers causing a distraction. I liked when they came by to look at my paintings. The police had my attention, though. Perhaps they were trying to blend into the background, but as far as I was concerned, they weren't succeeding.

Out of the corner of my eye, I spotted Detective Pierce Meyer walking toward me. I hoped he was coming to share good news.

"Good morning," he said when he approached.

I wiped the paint off my hands on a nearby rag. "Hello. You're back. I hope that's because you found the killer."

Spotting my appearance in the mirrored aviator sunglasses he wore gave me pause. Strands of hair fell from my ponytail and I could seriously use a swipe of lipstick. Pierce looked handsome, though, in his khaki pants and white polo shirt.

An amused expression came over his face. "Not exactly."

Why was he smirking at me like that?

"You have a little something on your cheek." He pointed.

I wiped my cheek and looked at my finger. "Number eight-six-two. Clear Day is the name. I use it to paint the sky." I pointed at the painting on the easel by the trailer.

He studied the canvas. "You're great with the stippling."

"You paint?" Hiding the excitement in my voice was impossible.

"I took a class in college." A hint of a smile touched his lips.

I couldn't hold back a smile. It wasn't often someone mentioned brush techniques. Though the conversation was pleasant, I couldn't help but wonder why he was here. Did he have more questions for me?

"So what can I do for you this morning, Detective Meyer?" I asked.

He moved closer to the painting of the old, weather-beaten farmhouse and peered down. After studying it a few moments, he focused his attention on me again. "How did you get that cut on your hand?"

I looked at my right hand. Did he think that was a cut from the murder weapon?

"I broke the glass jar I use to clean my paintbrushes." I stammered the words. I knew I sounded suspicious when I did that.

"Did you know Evan well? A few people said you were unhappy with the lack of security here. Did you have words with him about that?"

My heart rate spiked and my stomach twisted into a knot. "I hadn't asked him about security yet. That was why I went to speak with him," I said. Who had told him I was upset with Evan?

"So you didn't speak with him last night?" Detective Meyer asked.

"Only earlier, when he stopped by Shar's booth. Look, everyone probably had words with Evan. He was kind of a . . . how should I put this?" I asked.

"He was a bit of a pain?" the detective asked.

"Yes, that's a polite way of saying it," I said.

The detective peered around our surroundings. He seemed lost in thought. When he turned his attention back to me, he asked, "Is there anything else you're forgetting to tell me?"

"If anything, you should speak with Shar Pricket. Evan was nitpicking and wanted her to move her table back two inches. That made her angry and she said she wanted to knock him into next week." I pumped my fist for emphasis.

The slightest of smiles spread across the detective's face. I hated to notice how handsome he was at a time like this, but to be honest, the thought had crossed my mind several times.

"By the way, I had this cut two days ago." I pointed.

Maybe a bit too much self-confidence laced my words. I'd found my courage. In my opinion, the detective shouldn't consider me a suspect. Yes, I'd found the body, but I wasn't the only one in the area. After all, Caleb had been there, although he seemed far too nice to be a killer.

"I'll make sure to speak with Ms. Picket again," Detective Meyer said. "Please call if you think of anything else."

"I will," I said.

As the detective walked away, I felt the sensation that someone was watching me. When I glanced over, I spotted Ruth peeking out at me through the little window of her trailer. She'd seen me talking with the detective, so she probably thought I was the prime suspect. Was everyone at the craft fair suspicious of me because I found Evan's body?

I was a bit surprised the craft fair would continue, even with the help of Evan's assistant, Max. He had certainly taken charge. In my mind, it wasn't business as usual, though. Especially since the police were back. Being asked so many questions made me uncomfortable. I wanted to find the killer so that I wouldn't be under suspicion. Perhaps I should look into Evan's background. With any luck, I could make a list of suspects. Plus, find the killer's motive for murder.

Right now, I had to push thoughts of murder and robbery from my head and get to work. A couple of more days and the craft fair would be over. I'd lose my chance to sell paintings. After putting my work out for display, I picked up Van from the trailer and put him in his carrier. Okay, maybe it was actually a pink purse. In my defense, he liked sitting in it while I worked. He either took naps, watched people, or oversaw my painting to make sure I did it right.

What would I do with the portrait of the woman? There was only one thing *to* do. I would put it out and see what happened. I'd almost convinced myself that last night had been nothing more than a dream. The painting was most certainly not haunted.

With Van in my arms, I went back into the trailer. The portrait was where I'd left it. What did I think? That it would move on its own? Nevertheless, it was probably best if I sold it. I would always think about seeing the woman again if I kept the thing.

I eased over to the painting as if the woman would jump out at me.

"Van, I'm being silly." I set him down so I could carry the painting outside. "I'll be right back."

As I picked up the painting, the blanket I'd

tossed over it slipped and fell to the floor. I wanted to avoid looking at her, but I couldn't stop myself. Yes, it still seemed as if she was watching me.

"Stop staring at me," I said.

She didn't stop, though, so I hurried outside with her. I placed her next to a painting of a man on a horse. Whew. At least I'd gotten the painting outside. Just looking at her sent shivers down my spine. I turned around to go back to the trailer.

"I don't like being next to him," a female voice said.

I whipped around to see who had spoken, but no one was nearby. Now I was not only seeing things but hearing them too. I looked at the painting again. Nothing had changed. She still had that same haunted expression.

Brushing off the incident, I went back into the trailer for Van. When I stepped out again, the woman's voice came from somewhere close. "Are you listening to me? I don't like being beside this man. The horse stinks too."

I didn't know what to think. Someone must be playing a joke on me. Van was back in his little carrier beside me as I settled in front of my easel and picked up a paintbrush. His ears perked up and he barked. I was pretty sure he had no idea who he was barking at either.

A horse? As far as I knew, there were no horses at the craft fair. Maybe I'd overheard a conversation and got the words wrong. There was no need to freak out, I reminded myself. I'd concentrate on painting. Today I wanted to capture a scene of the fair, with people enjoying themselves on a lovely summer day. A fresh canvas always relaxed me and that was what I needed right now. I never dreamed this craft fair would be so stressful.

It hit me: The only horse around that I knew of was in the painting next to the woman's portrait. It couldn't be possible, right? Was the portrait talking to me now? I'd officially lost it.

Thank goodness a few customers stopped by my booth. I even sold the painting with the garden full of pastel-colored flowers to a couple expecting their first child in a couple of months. They planned to add the art to the baby's nursery. That kept my mind off the strange portrait and the murder.

A few times throughout the day, I looked over at Ruth's booth. I wanted to speak with her, but we'd both been busy. I had a hasty lunch of peanut butter crackers, washed down with an RC Cola, and the afternoon flew by as people browsed and shopped. As the day was coming to an end, I hoped to talk with her about what had happened.

I'd finished up a painting by adding fluffy cotton clouds to the blue sky and was curious about any hidden images. Had a mysterious image been painted into this one too? There was only one way to find out. I picked up one of the jars I used to clean my brushes and held it up to my eye. I squinted with one eye shut and peered through the glass with the other. The glass almost fell from my hand when I spotted it. There was something hidden within the painting. And I hadn't put it there on purpose. How was this happening?

A dancing skeleton was in the picture with the pretty pink, yellow, and purple flowers surrounding it. I hadn't added it, so I couldn't understand how a spooky image had ended up in such a serene work of art.

I'd of course heard of artists adding hidden images, but never without knowing about it. Was my subconscious doing this? If so, why? I picked up the jar and placed it with the rest of my supplies. Out of the corner of my eye, I spotted Ruth.

"Ruth." I waved for her attention.

She acted as if she hadn't heard me, but I was almost sure she had. I stepped closer to her booth and called out again. Ruth looked over at me as if I was a mosquito buzzing around her head.

"Oh, hello, Celeste. How are you?" From Ruth's tone, I knew she was completely annoyed.

Maybe it was my imagination, but she'd seemed a bit standoffish ever since she'd seen me speaking with the detective.

"Things have been busy today. How are you handling this?" I asked.

She knew I meant the murder.

"Business was good today. I always handle that fine," she said with a smirk.

I had to press for more information from her. A tiny part of me wanted to know why she'd been sneaking into her trailer last night right after the murder. She'd looked as if she hoped no one noticed her.

"Did the police speak with you?" I pressed.

I knew they had because I'd seen them stop her this morning. Though they hadn't spoken long. Perhaps I should come right out and ask what they'd said.

"They asked if I saw anything," she said as she

moved around a plastic box full of assorted multi-colored beads.

"*Did* you see anything?" I asked.

Apparently, that question captured her attention enough for her to actually focus on me.

"I saw nothing. I'd been in my trailer," she snapped.

"But I saw you going back into your trailer."

"Well, sure, after I heard the ruckus. I just came out to see what was causing such a commotion."

Was she being truthful? I didn't know her well, so I had no idea.

"It's tragic what happened," I said.

"Yes, well, it shouldn't come as a surprise to anyone with the way Evan treated people. I suppose someone finally got sick of his behavior." She showed no emotion.

"Yes, but I can't imagine someone killing him," I said.

She shrugged. "It happens."

"I certainly didn't expect anyone to kill him."

"Oh look, you have a customer." She pointed.

Lucky for Ruth, a woman wearing a white T-shirt with a cartoon drawing of a fawn-colored Chihuahua printed across the front had stopped by my booth and was smiling at a painting of Van. I had more questions, but I had to talk with the fellow Chihuahua lover. For now, I would have to postpone asking.

CHAPTER 6

Travel trailer tip 6:
When living in a travel trailer with your furry
companions, remember to make a space they can
call home. Adding a comfy bed and toys will
make them less anxious about traveling.

I moved back to my booth to help the customer. When I peeked back at Ruth, our eyes made contact, but she quickly looked away, as if nervousness and anxiety had set in. However, that could be her way of dealing with the stress of the murder.

I tried to push the supposedly haunted portrait of the woman on the man looking at my paintings, but he wasn't interested. I realized it was bad of me to try to give someone else my problem. I would have to keep the painting.

I hated to destroy a piece of art. What else could I do with it? Once again, I was acting as if I knew for sure the thing was haunted. Luckily, I sold a small painting to the man. He was quite taken with a painting of a fisherman wading in a stream near a covered bridge. I wondered if it had a hidden

image. I'd forgotten to check that one. I sat down
on the folding lawn chair in front of my trailer. I
also had an umbrella to keep the sun away. I took
skin care seriously and tried to limit my time in the
sun. Something I hadn't thought about in my
younger days.

As I sat there looking out over the crowd, I spotted Shar and Carly walking together. They must
have felt someone watching them because they
looked my way. They said something to each other
and crossed the path heading toward me. I wasn't
sure why, but an uneasy feeling came over me. I
tried to act casual as they approached. Maybe they
weren't coming to talk to me at all. After all, I
barely knew them. As they neared my booth, I
stood from the chair with Van in my arms.

"Good afternoon," I said when they stepped
close to my display table.

"Has the detective talked with you?" Shar asked.

Wow. She got right to the point.

"Yes, I spoke with him last night and again a
short time ago," I said. "You do realize I was the
one who found Evan."

"Yes, that's what we heard," Shar said.

"We just wanted to make sure you knew that
Shar didn't mean what she said about Evan," Carly
said.

"I was just angry." Shar pinched her brows together in a scowl.

Well, murderers were angry—that was why they
murdered.

"I understand." I certainly wasn't going to argue
with them.

"Did you tell the detective what I said?" Shar asked.

There was no way I would admit to that. "I just told him that I found the body and that was all I knew," I said.

See, I hadn't technically lied to Shar, I'd just avoided answering her question.

They watched me for a bit longer.

"Well, with any luck the police will stop poking around soon and leave us alone," Carly said.

That was a strange statement. She could have said, "With any luck they will find the killer soon." I hoped that was what she meant. The longer they stood in front of me, the more uneasiness settled between us.

"Oh, I wouldn't trust them if I were you," a female voice said.

I spun around. No one was behind me. Ruth was at her booth helping a customer. Van was looking in the direction of the paintings. Had he heard it too?

Carly cleared her throat. I turned around, focusing my attention on Shar and her again. They didn't mention that they'd heard anyone. Was I the only who'd heard the woman? The stress of finding a dead body was really getting to me now.

"Good luck with your booth today," Carly said with a fake smile.

"We'll see you around." Shar waved.

They turned and walked away. As they passed Ruth's booth, they exchanged a look with her. What were they up to?

I knew that Shar, Carly, and Ruth didn't like Evan,

but what about others? Max Stone had worked closely with Evan, so what did he think of him? I'd have to ask some questions. Maybe later, when the fair had stopped for the evening, I'd track him down. Oh, no—what if I found him with a knife sticking from his neck too? The thought sent a shiver down my spine.

In my mind, I had a suspects list already. Maybe I was being too suspicious of everyone. Caleb Ward happened to be right there when I found the body. Why had he been there? Maybe because he was the killer. He might be handsome and charming, but that didn't mean he couldn't be the killer. There were the vendors . . . Ruth, Shar, and Carly. They'd seemed mad enough for murder. Maybe not so much Ruth, but definitely Shar and Carly. Then again, I'd seen Ruth coming back to her trailer last night. She had acted awfully strange.

Something else was on my mind too. Something I had to get to the bottom of before I officially labeled myself bonkers. Where had the woman's voice come from? I didn't want to admit it, but it seemed as if it had come from the painting. Which still seemed as if she was watching me. What if I asked the painting a question? Would it answer me? I wouldn't want anyone to see me talking to a painting.

Movement caught my attention and I spotted Caleb and his beautiful German shepherd. The muscular dog marched along beside him. His black-and-tan coat gleamed, and his perky ears stood at attention as they drew near.

Caleb approached me. "Celeste, I'd like you to meet Gum Shoe."

The dog sat next to Caleb with his dark, almond-shaped, expressive eyes focused on me.

"Gum Shoe? That's quite an interesting name. Why Gum Shoe?"

Caleb rubbed his furry friend's head. "I just thought it sounded good."

"Nice to meet you, Gum Shoe," I said. "He's about a hundred of Van."

Caleb laughed. "Yeah, I bet they would be good friends, though. Gum Shoe gets along well with all dogs and most cats."

"Well, we should introduce them so they can play together." I reached down and rubbed Gum Shoe's head.

A good thing in Caleb's favor was that he was an animal lover like me. So that meant he couldn't be a murderer, right? He wouldn't be so nice to animals and mean to humans. However, what if Evan had made Caleb so furious he just lost control? I couldn't wrap my mind around that thought.

"Wait here and I'll get Van. He's taking a nap."

I hurried inside and retrieved Van. He opened his eyes, blinking several times. No doubt he wondered why I was waking him. He squinted as I took him into the bright sunshine.

"He's a bit sleepy right now."

"He's adorable," Caleb said.

Gum Shoe perked up when he spotted Van. I moved closer so they could sniff each other. Gum Shoe's ears stood up even taller. Van turned his attention away.

"He's still sleepy," I said.

"Maybe another time, when he's fully awake," Caleb said.

A customer walked up and was checking out my art.

"I'll let you go. Just let us know when Van wants a playdate." Caleb motioned for Gum Shoe to stand.

"Certainly." I waved.

Van barked as Gum Shoe walked away. Gum Shoe looked back at Van.

"Oh, now you want to play, when he has to leave?" I asked. "You'll have to wait until later."

CHAPTER 7

Travel trailer tip 7:
Keep extra flashlights and lanterns for times
when you need to check out the things that
go bump in the night.

The rest of the day was busy, so when evening came around, all I wanted to do was retire to my trailer and relax with Van. He had a dinner of his favorite chicken-flavored dog food. I had veggies and tofu that I'd bought from a food stall at the fair.

The woman's painting was with the others in the storage container on the rack my brothers had installed on the back of the Shasta. I hadn't brought the painting into the trailer tonight. Just in case anything strange happened. I was in bed, trying to fall asleep, when Van sat up. I opened one eyelid and spotted his oversize ears perked even more than usual. Voices carried from outside my trailer. It sounded as if they were close.

When Van barked, I scooped him up and went over to the door. I eased it open just a bit. About half a dozen people were standing around. Most wore their pajamas. Obviously, something else had happened. I hoped it wasn't another murder. Dressed in gray sleep shorts and a pink sleep tank, I stepped out into the warm night air. Ruth, wearing a light blue robe, stood nearby with a tall, gray-haired man, and I headed over to ask what had happened. I recognized him as the food vendor who sold kettle corn.

"Ruth, is everything okay?" I asked.

She turned around to face me. "No, everything isn't okay."

"I'll talk to you later, Ruth," the man said as he walked away.

Once he'd gone, Ruth said, "Someone had money taken again."

"Oh, no. Who was it this time?" I asked.

"It was Carly."

"That's terrible," I said. "Did she call the police?"

"Yes, I believe she's speaking with them now," Ruth said.

Had Detective Meyer returned to investigate? Yes, I thought he was handsome, but I definitely didn't want to speak with him. Raised voices sounded from a number of booths around us. Tempers were mounting at the craft fair. People were saying they wanted to leave before they became a robbery victim or even worse . . . murder. The police had asked us to remain until they had spoken to everyone. That could take a while.

"You'd better watch your money," I said.

Maybe I'd said that wrong. My tone had sounded more like a threat than a well-meaning warning.

Ruth eyed me up and down. "I'd better go now."

"I just meant . . ."

She turned and walked away. However, she passed by her trailer and kept going down the path. Her behavior had certainly changed since the first time we'd spoken. Undoubtedly, she suspected me as the criminal. I supposed there was nothing more to do, so I'd just go back to my trailer.

Now I was on edge even more. I'd love to hear the details of the latest crime from Carly. Though I assumed she was busy talking with the police. I supposed a quick stroll down to her booth wouldn't hurt. Or would it? Was it safe to walk around here at night? Maybe I should think better of doing something like that. I knew everyone would want answers about why there had been so much crime plaguing the craft fair.

I decided to take a walk toward Carly's booth. It wasn't as if I was going to an isolated area. Other people would be around. I was surprised law enforcement didn't have officers stationed around the fairgrounds.

"Let's take a little walk, Van," I said while cradling him in my arms.

The area became more congested as I neared Carly's booth. Just a few more steps and I spotted her. She wasn't alone. Detective Meyer stood in front of her. They were involved in what looked like a serious conversation. Coming over here was probably a bad idea. I didn't want him to see me. He'd wonder what I was doing. Plus, it would remind him that I was at the scene of the murder too.

The detective looked up. When we made eye contact, I felt a rush of adrenaline. Where could I hide? I needed to get out of there right now.

I turned around and hurried back down the path toward my trailer. I didn't want to look back for fear of making eye contact with the detective again. After a few seconds, I sensed someone walking behind me. With the recent murder this made me a bit nervous. When I peered over my shoulder, the detective was right behind me. Oh no. There was no way I could act as if I hadn't seen him.

"Ms. Cabot, how are you?" he asked as he grew closer.

I stopped and faced him.

"Fine." I tried to sound confident, but I knew there was nervousness in my voice.

"I guess you heard what happened tonight." He gestured over his shoulder.

"I heard that money was taken again. Do you think this is connected to the murder?" I asked.

He studied my face. "I'm not sure if there's a connection, but we're looking into everything."

"That's good to know." I rubbed Van's head so he wouldn't become restless.

"I've been thinking about that night . . ." He didn't finish the sentence.

He peered over my shoulder and I turned, spotting Caleb. He looked as if he'd been walking in our direction but thought better of it. Caleb turned and headed in the opposite direction.

The detective said, "If you'll please excuse me, Ms. Cabot, I need to speak with someone."

"Certainly," I said.

As he hurried around me, I sniffed the scent of a spicy aftershave.

"You can call me Celeste," I called out in his wake.

He offered no response. Van barked.

"Well, what do you think of that, Van?"

He tilted his head at me.

"Yes, it is interesting," I said.

I often answered for Van based on what I thought he was thinking. Okay, it was more like what I wanted his answers to be, but if Van could talk, we'd probably agree on a lot. The detective disappeared around the same corner where Caleb had gone just seconds before. Caleb had looked as if he'd been trying to get away from the detective. If only I could be a fly on the wall and overhear their conversation.

Light glowed from the window on the side of my trailer. I'd left the light on when I rushed out. As I drew near the trailer, I thought I saw a shadow move inside. Panic raced through me. Someone was in my trailer. I bet this was the person who was stealing money from the vendors. Little did they know I had my cash on me. After what had happened, I wasn't going to leave money inside. I wondered if I should get the police right away. I wanted to make sure this wasn't just my imagination.

My heart thumped in my ears as I moved closer to the trailer. Van shivered in my arms as I held him tight. What would I do if the intruder came out and caught me? What if this was the killer? It could be the same scenario that had played out for Evan. Perhaps the killer had been in Evan's trailer trying to steal money when Evan caught him. This was too dangerous. I needed to get the police right away.

Just as I turned around, I saw the ghost through the window. She looked as solid as any living person I'd ever seen. It was the woman from the portrait again. The one I'd seen last night. Maybe I was losing my mind. If it hadn't been for the customer who'd told me the painting was haunted, I certainly would've thought that by now. However, someone else had seen this as well. I didn't know what to do. Should I go ask her what she was up to? *Hello, Ghost, why are you haunting me?*

That sounded ridiculous, but maybe it was a good idea. Van barked as he watched the woman too. She paced inside the trailer, as if maybe she was waiting for me. I should just open the door and see what happened.

I didn't want Van to be scared, but I couldn't let him down either. As I wrapped my hand around the doorknob and twisted with one hand, I clutched Van close to my body with the other. When I inched the door open, the ghost was right there. I had no other explanation than to say she truly was a ghost. I couldn't call her a figment of my imagination. That just wasn't possible because the customer had seen her too. Plus, Van watched her as he would any living person. She stopped and looked directly at me. Our eyes met. Van didn't make a peep. Usually he barked at strangers, but not this time. He was probably stunned too.

"Hello," I said cautiously.

"Finally you're going to speak to me," she said around a sigh.

"I didn't know I was supposed to talk to you." I said as I inched closer.

"Well, when someone speaks to you, don't you think you should talk back?" She lifted her head in a regal manner.

"Yes, I suppose I should. Who are you?" I asked.

"My name is Elizabeth Mallory. And you are?"

I'd assumed she already knew my name.

"Celeste Cabot." The words came out as more of a question than a fact.

"A pleasure to make your acquaintance, Celeste." She smiled, showing lovely white teeth with a slight gap in the front.

"Likewise. Um, how did you get in my trailer?" I asked.

"You painted me, of course. And now here I am," she said with a wave of her hand.

I painted her to life? How was that possible? Van and I exchanged a look. We were both wondering how she'd gotten here.

"How do you know I painted you?" I pressed my back against the trailer's wall. It was the farthest I could stand from her without actually leaving the trailer.

"I don't know how you do it, but you do it," she said.

I closed my eyes, wondering if she'd disappear. Nope. She remained right there in front of me when I opened my eyes again.

"Are you a figment of my imagination?" I asked.

"I'm completely real. I was one hundred percent a living person. Now I suppose I'm just a spirit." Elizabeth sat primly on the stool, clasping her hands together and resting them on her lap.

There had to be a reason for her sudden appearance in my life.

"Is there something I can help you with?" I asked.

"That's a difficult question. I'm not sure why I am here." She remained stoic, with her posture at attention.

"I didn't bring you here on purpose," I said.

"You're the one who drew me and that's why I am here."

"So this is essentially my problem?"

This was crazy. The craziest thing I'd ever experienced. And with my family, I'd experienced a lot of wacky stuff. We were silent, both fixated on each other. I was at a loss for words.

"You don't have any clues that I could use to figure out why you're here?" I asked.

She shook her head. "Not a clue."

"Can you give me more information about who you are?" I asked.

"I was born in 1852. And I was married at the age of eighteen. I had six children. A very good life." The bottom of her ivory-colored dress swooshed as she shifted on the stool.

"That doesn't give me much to go on," I said.

"Are you talking to your dog?" a male voice called out.

I rushed over to the window to find Caleb standing right outside. He'd heard me through the open window. Thank goodness I had Van to use as an excuse for the talking. After picking him up, I opened the door and stepped outside the trailer.

"Yes, I was talking to my dog. I do that often. He doesn't talk back, of course," I said with a nervous

laugh. "Well, only if I make up the words for him."
I was rambling. A sure sign of nervousness.

Thank goodness Caleb laughed. If I sounded
nervous, my explanation would be the recent
events around the craft fair. Technically, that was
true.

I looked over my shoulder. The ghost was gone.
That was more unsettling than if she'd still been
there. Where had she gone to now? Back into the
painting? I concentrated on Caleb again. "So what
brings you by?" I asked.

Van wiggled in my arms as if he wanted to get
down.

"I just stopped by to see if you're okay after
everything that happened. I know it's a pretty
stressful situation."

"That's nice of you to think of me. Thank you,"
I said.

I placed Van on the ground and held on to his
leash. He went over to Caleb and sniffed his leg.

"Is it all right if I pet him?" Caleb asked. "Gum
Shoe was sleeping, so I left him in our trailer."

"Absolutely. Just make sure you stretch out your
hand first to let him know that you're friendly. It's
a little scary for him when people just kind of
lunge at him."

"That's understandable. Especially with his size.
I wouldn't like a giant reaching down for me either."

I laughed. "Yes, it is scary."

Van sniffed Caleb's hand and allowed Caleb to
scratch his ears. Within seconds, Van rolled over
onto his back for a belly rub. As Caleb rubbed Van,
I noticed his hands. He had cuts on his fingers.

That stood out to me because the detective had asked me about my cut. Had the detective noticed the cuts on Caleb's hands?

As a woodsmith, Caleb worked with knives, so that would be an excuse. However, at what stage was he in his career? If he'd been doing this a while, I'd figure he'd be cut free. I'd have to ask an expert in that kind of thing. I suppose accidents happened. Though now the discovery made me a little uneasy. After all, I'd seen Caleb at Evan's right after the murder. Now he had an injury? Those two things would possibly make him a suspect.

When I realized Caleb had caught me checking out his hands, my anxiety spiked. I picked up Van and held him close to me. I didn't want a murderer around my dog. Was I was jumping to conclusions? Caleb seemed like a nice guy. Not to mention he was handsome. I tried to ignore his good looks, but it was hard not to notice the tiny dimple that appeared when he unleashed his lopsided smile. The small scar above his right eyebrow drew attention to his big, sapphire-colored eyes.

"I got the cuts from working with wood," he said.

"I assumed," I said.

Did I sound natural when I answered him? Did I sound nervous? My voice was probably shaky. Caleb shoved his hands into his jean pockets. Probably so I would stop looking at them. It was too late now. I'd already seen them.

"There is one other reason I stopped by this evening," Caleb said.

Now my anxiety spiked all over again. "Oh yeah? What other reason?" I asked with a shaky voice.

"I thought maybe you'd like to have dinner with me."

I didn't know what to say. I thought he was nice, and if he wasn't a murderer, I would probably be interested in him. I suppose if I went to dinner with him I could question him more about Evan.

I could just insist we go somewhere public, with lots of people who would see me. More importantly, I'd go nowhere alone with him. That would be safe, right?

"When did you have in mind for dinner?" I asked.

"How about tomorrow evening?"

"I can meet you somewhere," I said. That way I wouldn't be alone in a vehicle with him.

"That'll work. Where would you like to go?" he asked.

"There's a little café nearby if that's all right with you?"

My Aunt Patsy owned the place. She would take no funny business from Caleb if he was up to something. And I'd be among people who knew and cared about me.

CHAPTER 8

Travel trailer tip 8:
Remember not to leave food out so as not to attract
animals. Running into a bear at breakfast is not
a good way to start your day.

Since I hadn't expected to have a date for the evening, I hadn't brought an appropriate outfit. Even though it was just my aunt's little café around the corner, I felt a paint-stained T-shirt and jeans were probably a bit too casual . . . and slobby. Aunt Patsy would have a fit if she saw me dressed like that for a date.

My home was a short drive away, so I decided to make a quick trip by my place for a change of clothing. Plus, my mother had agreed to watch Van while I went out with Caleb. Going out with Caleb? That sounded strange. Was I really having dinner with someone I suspected could be the murderer?

As I pulled into the driveway of my family's modest, red-brick ranch home, I noticed that the mailbox had fallen off its post again. Although my father and brothers were whizzes when it came to fixing vehicles, they couldn't seem to get the mailbox to stay put.

My mom came out to meet me wearing jeans and a T-shirt covered by an apron that clearly told me she had been cooking spaghetti sauce. "Have you lost your ever-lovin' mind?" she asked as she picked up Van.

"I know it sounds crazy, but I figure I can ask him questions. I'll know if he's guilty."

"I doubt he's going to confess, Celeste. He'd only do that right before he murders you. Once that happens, it won't matter if he confessed to you," she said.

"I see your point." I handed her Van's bag of toys, food, and treats. "Though I have it all planned. We're going to Aunt Patsy's place. There's no way he'd try anything around her."

"How long is Van staying with me?" She eyed the tote bag.

"Just a few hours. Why?"

My mother pulled out the six toys I'd picked out for Van. "Oh, no reason."

Screaming and yelling came from somewhere out back. My mother and I raced to the noise. My father and brothers were stomping on something in the backyard. Smoke billowed from whatever they were attacking.

My mother and I ran toward them.

"What in blue blazes is going on out here?" my mother asked as she wiped her forehead with a dish towel.

"Dad tried to start a fire to burn some trash while wearing his work gloves. He'd cleaned the gloves with gasoline," my brother Stevie said.

"How many times have I told you no fires?" My mother blew the hair that had fallen from her bun out of her eyes.

My father was a man of few words. He reached down and picked up his charred gloves. After a quick assessment, he placed them back on his hands.

"Well, back to work," he said, walking away as if nothing had happened.

My father's birthday was next week. I supposed I'd buy him new gloves as a present.

"And don't you dare buy him new gloves," my mother said, as if reading my mind. "He doesn't deserve a new pair if he's just going to set them on fire."

She said this, but I knew she'd probably buy him a new pair tomorrow. We were used to my father's antics by now. He wasn't the only one in the family who acted this way, though. My brothers, cousins, uncles . . . they all had their share of not-so-great ideas. Now that the excitement was over, we headed inside. Walking through the kitchen, I enjoyed the aroma of homemade tomato sauce with fresh basil while trying to ignore the messy red splotches on the walls near the stove. The window on the oven allowed a view of the baking pie. My mother's famous lavender blueberry peach pie. She'd won a blue ribbon at the county fair with that recipe. My dad and brothers were in for a tasty meal.

Mama Cabot's Lavender Blueberry Peach Pie

Mama says she makes her own pie dough, but we all know she cheats sometimes and buys pre-made from the grocery store. We'll let that remain her little secret.

½ cup all-purpose flour
1 cup sugar, plus extra for sprinkling
Zest and juice of ½ lemon
1½ teaspoons vanilla extract
1 teaspoon lavender extract
½ teaspoon cinnamon
4 cups sliced peaches
2 cups blueberries
2 pie pastries for a 9-inch pie
2 tablespoons butter
1 large egg

Preheat oven to 425 degrees F.

Stir flour, 1 cup sugar, lemon zest and juice, vanilla, lavender extract, and cinnamon together. Set aside.

Mix together sliced peaches and blueberries and combine with dry ingredients.

Spoon into pastry-lined pie pan and dot with butter.

Place 4 pie pastry strips about 1 inch apart over the filling. Weave the remaining strips perpendicular. Trim off overhanging dough. With a fork, crimp the pie dough around the edge of the pan.

Whisk egg with 1 teaspoon of water. Brush egg wash over lattice dough and edges of the pie with a pastry brush.

Sprinkle top with sugar.

Bake for 30 minutes until crust is brown.

"I'll be back later," I said, heading through the living room with a wave of my hand. I had twenty minutes to get to the diner.

My mother hurried in front of me. "Not so fast." She blocked the front door by stretching her arms out to the sides.

"What did I do?" I asked.

"I'm worried about you, Celeste. It's not every day someone discovers a murder victim. Plus, I have no idea who you're meeting for dinner."

"He has a booth at the fair," I said. "He makes hand-carved replicas of old-timey toys and the cutest birdhouses you ever saw. You'd like them, Mom."

My mother's eyebrow raised. "So he's an artist. What else does he do?"

"He's just an artist." I reached around her for the doorknob.

She blocked me with her hip. "What's his name?" she asked.

Uh-oh. I had hoped to escape before she asked for his name. She'd probably drag out her old laptop, and as soon as she got it fired up, she'd Google him. No need, though. I'd already tried it and found nothing on him. Not even a Facebook account. Lying to her and giving a fake name wouldn't work either. She sniffed out my lies like a bloodhound on the trail of a crime.

I twisted the doorknob and opened the door slightly. "Caleb Ward."

She didn't budge.

"You're much stronger than you look." I grunted as I tried to open the door.

"Caleb Ward," she repeated.

I knew she was repeating the name so she could remember it.

"Okay, I have to go," I said.

This time she didn't stop me. "Be careful out there," she called as I rushed toward my truck.

I'd left the trailer at the fair. It was tough driving around with the thing attached to my vehicle. I was happy with my decision to purchase it, though, and my family had done a beautiful job of renovating it. Now I could travel around to craft fairs all over the region. In the summers I could even head north.

About ten minutes later, I arrived at Patsy's Paradise Café. Pictures of palm trees flanked the diner's name on the large sign on the little building. I wasn't sure what kind of car Caleb drove, so I had no idea if he had arrived. The diner's décor was eclectic to say the least. The surrounding landscape figured all types of lawn decorations. Plastic flamingos, gnomes, and fake palm trees gave an atmosphere of whimsy that reflected my aunt's personality. I parked the truck and headed inside the diner.

"Celeste!" Patsy called out as soon as I stepped inside.

Her greeting brought a smile to my face. Patsy's hair was swept up toward the sky in a cone shape. It was the exact color of the maple syrup she served with fluffy pancakes.

"Good evening, Patsy." I waved.

She gestured with a tilt of her head toward one of the booths by the window. Her palm-tree earrings swayed with the motion. Caleb was already sitting there. His stare was focused on me. A huge smile spread across my face. Butterflies danced in my stomach. He looked even more handsome than I remembered. Appearance-wise, he reminded me of a modern-day James Dean. Caleb had a boy next door quality, but underneath was he hiding bad boy behavior? Momentarily, I felt guilty for even thinking he might be involved with the murder. I headed for the table. He stood as I neared.

Caleb wore jeans and a pullover shirt. Like me, he had dressed casually, taking the time to wear something that didn't scream artist working. His blue eyes sparkled under the artificial light and his smile beamed.

"You made it," he said.

Had he thought I wouldn't show up?

"Yes, and you're here too," I said around a laugh.

"Is this table all right?" he asked with a gesture of his hand.

Did he know this was the booth I always sat at? Had Patsy told him?

"Yes, it's perfect."

"I thought this booth had the best view of the parking lot," he said.

I laughed. "The food makes up for the lack of scenery."

After I sat down, he slid onto the seat across from me. "I'm guessing you have some connection to Patsy."

He focused his attention on the counter, where Patsy was busy at the register. Oh no. What had she done? Should I admit that she was my aunt or keep quiet? I supposed he would find out eventually if we continued to see each other. I might as well get the truth out there. I picked up a menu and handed it to Caleb.

"Patsy's my aunt on my father's side. Plus, she's my boss. Sometimes, that is." I wanted him to see me as an artist, not a waitress, so I downplayed my part-time work at the diner. "I mean, I occasionally help her out here."

"I thought I saw a resemblance," he said. "So tell me, what's the best thing on the menu?"

"Hands down, the burgers. Though if you want thick, you won't get that here. She makes the meat so thin, it practically crumbles apart. Now normally, I would say that's a bad thing, but in this case, it's just . . . magical. The flavor is magical."

"Wow. After that description, how could I order anything else?" He placed the menu down.

As if on cue, Patsy appeared next to our table. "What can I get you two good-looking dolls tonight?"

"We've decided on burgers, Patsy," I said.

"With cheese?" she asked.

"Cheese for me," Caleb said.

"And none for Celeste. Diet Coke for Celeste and . . ." She eyed Caleb up and down. "Sweet tea for you."

He quirked an eyebrow. "Yes, that's right."

Patsy turned like a twirling ballerina and headed for the kitchen.

"How did she know that?" Caleb asked.

"Like I said, things are almost magic around here."

He chuckled. "I guess so."

Now that the ordering was complete, I realized we'd have to find something to talk about. There had been two seconds of silence and I was already panicking. I supposed there was no real reason to freak out just yet. After all, we were both artists and we could always discuss that.

"You're a woodworker?" I asked.

"You're a painter?" he asked.

We spoke at the same time. Next, we laughed at the same time.

"You go first," Caleb said.

"I saw some of your work and I think it's fantastic," I said. "I especially love your toys with the moving parts. They're so clever."

His cheeks turned a light shade of pink. "Thank you. I appreciate that you took the time to check out my stuff."

The conversation was coming a lot easier than I'd thought.

"Oh, I almost forgot," he said, jumping up from the table.

"Is something wrong?" I asked.

"Wait right here." He held up his index finger and raced for the door.

I wondered what this was all about. I nervously folded a napkin while I waited. A few seconds later, Caleb came back in holding a pink-paper-wrapped package with a white ribbon secured in a bow around it. He'd bought me a gift?

Caleb slipped into the booth across from me. "I brought you something."

"Wow. That is incredibly thoughtful. You didn't have to do that."

"Oh, I know I didn't have to do it, but I wanted to. Open it."

My stomach danced as I picked up the package and slowly slid off the paper. The small, gold-painted wooden frame was perfect.

"I know it's not big, but I didn't have time to make a larger one for you."

"It's perfect," I said. "I didn't bring you a gift."

"Talking to you is gift enough," Caleb said.

Heat rushed to my cheeks. "I have a canvas I painted of Van. It will fit perfectly in the frame."

Caleb beamed. "That sounds perfect."

After placing the frame on the table, we went back to conversation. I couldn't stop glancing over at the frame. The gift was one of the nicest things anyone had ever made for me.

"I've been excited about the craft fair. But now it's turned into a crime scene," I said. "That might put a damper on things."

"Perhaps things will pick up once people realize there was a murder there. It might attract attention and people'll want to come."

"That's a bit morbid," I said, toying with the salt and pepper shakers. They were in the shape of a pair of flamingos.

"How have you been feeling?" Caleb leaned back and put his arm across the back of the booth, looking relaxed.

"Anxious, of course, but at least I have my painting to help relieve anxiety and stress. That's always been therapeutic for me." I ran my finger along the wooden frame.

Our conversation seemed to go smoothly, but I had to remember the reason for being here. I needed to ask Caleb questions about himself and why he had been at Evan's trailer that night.

Patsy brought our food, and we both dug in to the juicy burgers. After swallowing a bite, I said, "You were going to visit Evan that night. Why?"

I just had to come out and ask the question. There was no way around it.

He looked at me and picked up a French fry, dipping it into a pool of ketchup on his plate. "I needed to discuss some of the policies they have at the craft fair."

"Like what?" I asked.

"It's just that he changed a lot of things after we arrived. I expected one thing and he would do another, like where he had my booth and the time limit on when we could have things out. I was just generally unhappy with everything."

"Do you think a lot of people were unhappy with him?" I asked.

"From what I heard, yes, there were a lot of people not happy with the way he was running things," he said.

"So unhappy they would kill him?" I pressed.

He studied my face. "I suppose if the person was enraged like that, they might be set off by his behavior."

"An enraged person? I wonder who could be

that angry." I studied his face to see if there was any clue.

Who was I kidding? I wasn't an expert in analysis of people's emotions or behaviors. I would have to go about this another way. Just trying to read him and get him to confess to the crime wouldn't work. Besides, he seemed so nice. I certainly hoped I wasn't sitting with a killer.

Aunt Patsy brought over the check. She tried to get me not to pay for food every time I ate at the diner, but I insisted that if she wouldn't let me pay, I wouldn't make my famous peanut butter fudge for Christmas. It was her favorite. Sure, she was a great cook and all, but she said I had a magical touch with that stuff. I wasn't sure I did anything differently than she did, but if she liked it, that was all that mattered.

"I suppose we've taken up the booth for too long," Caleb said.

I realized the diner was packed. When had all the people come in? I'd been so engrossed in our conversation, I hadn't noticed.

"Yes, we should give someone else the table," I said.

Caleb grabbed the ticket. "I'll pay the check."

"Thank you, but I doubt Aunt Patsy will allow that," I said with a smile.

"Why'd she bring the check, then?" Caleb asked.

"She has her reasons," I said, keeping my theory to myself.

Caleb and I walked up to the register to pay. Aunt Patsy eyed Caleb as he approached. I knew she was full of questions. Luckily, because it was so busy, she wouldn't have the chance to ask much.

She smoothed her beehive hairdo. "How was everything?"

Aunt Patsy was my dad's sister. The expressive eyes and button noses gave away the family connection, but she'd made "slight adjustments" to her hair color. Normally she bleached it blond. Aunt Patsy called it a slight adjustment, but I called it night and day.

"Delicious." Caleb handed her cash.

She wasn't refusing money from him? Either that meant she didn't like Caleb, or she was testing to see if he'd offer to pay. Which of my theories would be correct? When she took the money, she looked down at his hand. Aunt Patsy had a thing about hands. She said you could always tell people's character by their hands. I didn't believe that to be true, but of course I didn't argue with her.

"Whoa, what happened to your hands? Were you on the losing end of a battle with a lion?" Aunt Patsy asked.

Caleb quickly moved his hand. "Oh, that. Yes, I was trying to bathe my sister's cat the other day."

That was odd. He'd told me they were injuries from his wood carvings. Why the change in story? Should I confront him about this? Now my anxiety returned.

Aunt Patsy smiled. "You'll have to be more careful next time."

He grinned. "Yes, I suppose I will."

What did he mean by that? The next time he murdered someone, he'd have to be more careful? It was time I ended this date.

"Have a good evening." Aunt Patsy winked.

She had no idea of the thoughts whirling in my mind.

Caleb gestured toward the door. "Shall we go?"

What if he asked me out again? I'd had a fabulous time and I didn't want him to be the killer. But I had to take into consideration the facts that I knew so far. If I continued to talk with him, I might find out more details, but I could also be putting my life in danger.

Night had settled around us now. Stars dazzled in the black sky with a slight summer breeze caressing my skin. The sweet smell of honeysuckle drifted across the air.

"Can I walk you to your truck?" he asked.

Thank goodness I had parked close and under a light. "It's right over there." I pointed.

"After you," he said with a smile.

Nerves danced in my stomach as I walked across the lot and over to my truck.

I stood beside the door with my keys in my hand. "Thank you for dinner."

"No, thank you for bringing me here. Now I have a new favorite place for burgers."

"Aunt Patsy will like that," I said.

I hoped I hadn't just brought a killer into my aunt's diner. My family would never let me live that down at the family Christmas each year.

"I'll see you at the fair?" Caleb asked.

"Of course," I said.

What was on his mind? Murder? I shivered at the thought.

"All right. I'll see you tomorrow," he said with wave.

He turned and walked toward his truck. Once I slid behind the steering wheel of my truck, I released a deep breath. That was one of the craziest things I'd ever done. It had looked like a simple date, but it was much more than that. When I glanced over, I noticed Caleb was still sitting in the parking lot. I'd prefer it if he left first. What was he waiting for?

Staying until he left the parking lot might seem weird, so I decided to pull out. I'd drive down the road and pull over so I could watch his next move. I'd try to hide so he wouldn't see my vehicle. That was if he was headed back toward the craft fair.

Anxiety crept back in. What if he went back into the café? He wouldn't do anything to Aunt Patsy, right? He had no motive to harm her. I was being paranoid. *Get ahold of yourself, Celeste.* All this murder talk was creeping me out. Never had I thought I'd be thrown into a murder investigation.

A few second later, I spotted Caleb's truck headed in my direction. Parked on the side of the road between a white van and a black sedan, my truck was probably still noticeable. I slid down in the driver's seat, hoping he wouldn't spot me. After counting to ten, I eased back up in the seat. Whew. Thank goodness he hadn't seen me. Now that I knew he'd left the café, I could go too. Crisis averted for now.

My phone rang. I jumped, not expecting the sound. When I saw the number on the screen, I knew I was in trouble.

"Aunt Patsy," I said when I picked up.

"Well, that was interesting," she said.

"What was so interesting about it?" I asked. "The fact that I had a date?"

"It is a bit of a surprise. What's the deal with that guy? I want to know all the details," she said.

"There's not much to tell," I said, knowing that wasn't the truth.

"I don't believe you," she said. "Where did you meet him?"

"At the craft fair." Did she notice the quiver of my voice? Technically, I had met Caleb at the fair. Aunt Patsy didn't need to know I'd met him over a dead body.

"What does he do?" she asked with suspicion in her voice.

"Well, he's a wood sculptor."

"That's it?" she asked. "What does he really do?"

"That's it," I said.

"There's not much money in that. How's he going to pay for food? Rent?"

"Well, he paid for food at your place. Speaking of which, why did you let him do that? I can't drop a penny on the floor without you chasing me down and giving it back."

"Because he ate food at my café."

"Yes, but you never let me pay."

"This was a different circumstance. I wanted to see if he actually had any money."

"Oh, that explains a lot," I said.

"You learn as you get older," she said.

Aunt Patsy still treated me like I was sixteen. At twenty-six years old, I was well on my way to being "older."

"There's just something about him," she said with a click of her tongue. "I can't quite put my finger on it. It's as if I've seen him somewhere before."

"Really?" I said, trying to sound casual. Now Aunt Patsy had me intrigued. "Maybe he's been to the café before and you just don't remember."

Though Caleb had said he'd never been to the café.

"No, I don't think that's where I've seen him. But let me tell you, if I've really seen him, I'll remember. My memory is like an elephant's. And when I remember where I've seen him, I'll make sure to tell you right away."

"I know you will," I said. "Aunt Patsy, I have to go now."

"You sound rushed. What's the problem?"

"Van is at my parents' and I don't want to put him through that for too long."

"You're right. You'd better hurry."

Celeste's Creamy and Soft Peanut Butter Fudge

Aunt Patsy can't get enough of this holiday favorite. It makes a great gift! Remember to store in an airtight container.

2 cups sugar
½ cup milk
1⅓ cups peanut butter
1 jar (7 ounces) marshmallow creme
1 teaspoon vanilla extract

Line an 8 x 8-inch square pan with parchment paper.

Combine sugar and milk and bring to a boil over medium heat. Once it comes to a boil, stir for three minutes.

Add peanut butter, marshmallow creme, and vanilla extract. Stir until blended.

Pour the fudge into pan and allow to cool. Place in refrigerator. Once firm, cut the fudge and remove from the pan.

CHAPTER 9

Travel trailer tip 9:
Keep a fire extinguisher handy in case you know
(or are) an accident-prone person.

I picked up Van from my parents' house. Luckily, my father hadn't caused any small disasters in the short time I'd been gone. It was only a matter of time, though, before he pulled another stunt. My mother didn't need to ask about my date because Aunt Patsy already had given her all the details. They'd been talking while Caleb and I ate our burgers. Apparently, Patsy gave my mother a play-by-play account.

"Patsy said he's handsome." My mother wiggled her eyebrows as we stood chatting on the front porch. My mom's red geraniums were in full bloom in the pots next to the steps.

My cheeks blushed.

"Aha. So he is handsome." My mother pointed at me.

I grabbed Van's bag. "I have to go. There's a painting I want to finish tonight."

"If you have another date with him, I expect more details. Maybe you can bring him around for dinner," my mother called out as I headed for my truck.

There was no way I would bring Caleb here for dinner. Not yet anyway. Van sat beside me on the seat as I drove back to the craft fair.

"Did you have a fun time at Nana and Papaw's house?" I asked.

Van covered his eyes with his paws as if he knew exactly what I'd asked.

"I know they're a bit kooky, but you gotta love them, right?"

I pulled my truck up to my assigned spot at the fair. A bit of relief washed over me now that I'd returned to my trailer. I didn't like leaving it full of paintings. I parked and gathered Van in my arms. He licked my face.

"Aw, thanks, sweetie," I said.

I paused at the trailer's door. The ghost could be standing there when I opened it. I mustered my courage and twisted the knob. To my relief, I saw no sign of the ghost. Maybe she'd decided not to return.

If only she'd asked, I could have warned her sooner that I was boring. There was nothing going on in this trailer other than painting. No glamorous parties or lively conversations. I released a sigh of relief and stepped into the trailer with Van. He raced over to his toys as if he was never so glad to see them.

"We weren't gone that long," I said as I took his stuff from the bag. "I know Nana and Papaw's house is a bit odd, but they love you bunches."

Just as I finished filling Van's dish with water and placed it on the floor, he barked. I looked up, and my gaze locked on the ghost. Elizabeth had had an outfit change. Her embroidered, chartreuse-colored dress had a capacious, bell-shaped skirt. Ringlet curls hung at the sides of her face peeking out from under her large white bonnet. A crocheted shawl was draped around her shoulders.

"Oh no," I said.

I raced over and picked up Van. She watched us as she stood by the door.

"You're back." I held Van to my chest.

"You didn't think I'd stay away, did you?" she asked.

"I was kind of hoping you would," I said.

"That's not very nice." She frowned.

"To be honest . . . Van is afraid of you."

Van wiggled from my arms.

"Van, no," I yelled.

He dashed over to the ghost and sat in front of her, wagging his tail as if they were best friends.

"Hello, sweet one, you're not afraid of me, are you?"

He rolled on his back and offered his belly for a rub.

"Van, you traitor," I whispered. "Fine, the truth is, I'm afraid of you."

"There's no need to be afraid. I'm not here to harm you."

"I don't know why you're here," I said.

"Well, that makes two of us. I told you, I don't know why I'm here."

What could I say now? Invite her to sit for a spell? It wasn't as if I could serve tea and scones.

"And I don't know what this is all about."

"You need to ask yourself why you painted my image. Where did you see me?" she asked.

"Before painting your portrait, I'd never seen you," I said.

"If you find the reason you painted me, maybe you can find the reason why I'm here."

I had to admit that made sense, although I had no idea how to begin to understand why I'd painted her image.

"I feel a sense of danger. Something tells me that you're in danger." Worry pinched between her dark eyebrows.

That wasn't what I wanted to hear.

"What kind of danger?" I asked with wide eyes.

Van had given up on getting a belly rub and was now observing my conversation with the ghost as if he was watching a tennis match.

"I think there's someone around here who wants to harm you," she said.

My stomach twisted. Could it be the killer? How would this ghost know that? Was she just trying to scare me? If so, it was working.

"Who wants to harm me?" I asked.

She moved from the door over to the tiny window and peered outside. "That I do not know."

"How do you know someone wants to hurt me?"

"That I do not know," she said again, still looking out the window.

Oh no. She was on repeat.

"Are your words stuck?" I asked.

She turned to face me and chuckled. "No, dear. I just don't know who wants to harm you. Before you ask why I don't know these things, I'll answer you. I don't have an answer for that either."

Van jumped up on the chair beside me and watched the ghost.

"What can I do to stay safe?" I asked.

"You said there's a killer?" she asked.

"Yes, someone was murdered here at the craft fair. They don't know who did it."

"That's terrible," she said.

"There are a few suspicious people."

I watched her face for a reaction.

"Who are these people?"

I fidgeted. "Actually, I went to dinner with one of them tonight."

"Why would you do that?" she asked.

"I thought it would be a good chance to ask him questions about the murder."

"And what did you find out?"

"Absolutely nothing." I paced across the tiny space to straighten a still life of summer fruit I'd hung on my wall.

"Who else do you suspect?"

"There are a couple of women who were extremely mad at the murdered man. They have booths here at the fair. Plus, the woman in the booth next to mine seemed unhappy with him. There's also someone stealing money from vendors here too."

"Sounds like this isn't a safe place," she said.

"I thought it was," I said.

A knock sounded on the door. Van barked. I picked him up to calm him down.

"Are you expecting a visitor?" Elizabeth asked.

"No," I whispered.

My heart rate increased. I didn't want to answer the door without knowing who was there. Not with a murderer on the loose.

"Would you like me to peek outside to see who's there?" she asked.

"You can do that?" I asked.

"I came from a canvas. Peeking out that door will be a piece of cake after that."

"That would be great. Thank you."

Van's body trembled as he growled. The ghost floated over to the door. Sometimes she floated and sometimes she walked. I wasn't sure about the rules of ghostly life. I watched in shock as she popped her head through the door.

After a few seconds, she pulled her head back through the door. Her hair wasn't even mussed. "A man is out there. I don't think you should answer the door. He could be trouble."

"What does he look like?" I asked.

"One minute, please," she said and popped her head through the door again.

The suspense was getting to me. A few more seconds and she returned. "Well? Can you tell me now?"

"A handsome man," she whispered, as if he would hear her.

Was it Caleb? The ghost stepped away from the door and back over to the window. I decided I would open the door. I eased the door open, as if that would prevent a killer from getting me.

Caleb wasn't the person at my door. It was the detective. The outside light highlighted the bourbon-colored streaks in his dark hair. Like the hidden images, the color was only visible in certain circumstances. Pierce wore a white dress shirt with the sleeves rolled up on his strong forearms, along with tan slacks. I assumed he had ditched the matching jacket and tie that went with his suit.

"Good evening, Ms. Cabot," said Pierce. "Did I come at a bad time?"

Surprisingly, Van wasn't barking at him. The detective smiled at him.

"I was getting ready to paint," I said, gesturing to the piece on the easel: the scene of the fair I'd been working on.

Yes, it was a hint I hoped he wouldn't stay long.

"You should be nicer to him," Elizabeth said. "He can keep you safe from the killer, no? Plus, he's easy on the eyes. You should invite him in."

The ghost stood closer to me now. I had no idea a ghost could be so chatty. Maybe I could have painted her without a mouth? No, that wouldn't be my style.

"Would you care to step outside to speak with me?" he asked.

Oh no. This wasn't looking good for me.

"Go on, talk with him." The ghost gestured.

With Van still in my arms, I stepped out of the trailer. My legs shook and I felt it a bit hard to breathe.

"Will he let me pet him?" the detective asked, reaching toward Van.

"Only if you let him sniff your hand first. Don't grab at him like you're going to harm me or him."

"He really is your little protector, isn't he?"

"People think chihuahuas like to bite, but that's not true. They're just scared and protective. Once they get to know you, they'll shower you with love. They're spunky and entertaining too."

Detective Meyer let Van sniff his hand, and Van allowed the detective to rub his back.

"He likes you," I said with a smile.

"Well, the feeling is mutual."

Okay, how bad could the detective be when clearly he liked dogs? Anyone who liked dogs was all right in my book. Plus, Van liked him too.

"What brings you by tonight, Detective?" I asked. "Has there been another robbery? Oh my gosh, has someone else been murdered?"

"No, don't worry, nothing else has happened. And you can call me Pierce."

First-name basis? Did he do that with everyone he thought was a murderer? Maybe he wanted to befriend me to get me to confess. I had already told him everything I remembered.

"As you know, I'm investigating the murder," he said.

Yes, I was well aware.

"I answered all your questions," I said.

"It was brought to my attention that you were with Mr. Ward tonight."

The words smacked me in the face. How had he found that out?

"We had dinner at my aunt's café. Is there something wrong with that?" I asked.

He studied my face. I sensed he wasn't telling me everything.

"When did you first see Caleb that night?"

The detective thought Caleb was the murderer? Of course, I had my suspicions too. Now that the detective had questioned me about Caleb, I didn't want it to be true.

"He just kind of popped up, I suppose."

"Do you think he could have already been there and you just thought he popped up?"

"No, not at all." I paused. "Yes, I suppose he could have already been there." Now the detective was putting even more doubts into my head. "Do you think Caleb killed Evan?"

"I didn't say that," he said.

He didn't have to say it. I read between the lines.

"Would you mind walking with me back to the scene to show me exactly where you first saw Caleb?"

I frowned. "Yes, if you think that will help. I'll leave Van in the trailer."

I remembered the ghost. Would she still be there? I eased the door open and peered inside.

"Are you looking for someone?" the detective asked.

"Um, no, just a habit."

Whew. I had to remember not to be so obvious about looking for my new ghost friend. Elizabeth was nowhere in sight. Was she hiding from the detective? I placed Van in his bed, although I figured he wouldn't stay there. He'd probably play with his toys. At least he seemed to like the ghost. If she came back while I was gone, he would probably ask her for another belly rub.

CHAPTER 10

Travel trailer tip 10:
Have the proper tools on hand. You never know
when you might have to do a repair.
Never leave home without your duct tape.

I locked the trailer door and turned to face the detective. "All set."

"I appreciate you helping me out," he said.

Like I had a choice. "You're welcome," I said.

The detective and I started down the path toward Evan's trailer. It was eerie now when I had to walk by the place. The gleaming moon provided the only source of illumination, washing the area in a white glow. Fireflies flickered in the dense trees along the edges of the dirt path. Their branches reached out, creating a canopy over the trail. The four-day craft fair would be over soon. Maybe I could put this all behind me. Who was I kidding? I'd never be able to completely put this behind me. I'd always remember what had happened.

We fell into step with each other. Well, the detective had to slow his steps to match mine. My short legs were no match for the stride of his long legs. There was no way our gait could have synced up.

"I didn't mean to alarm you by showing up here tonight," he said.

"I'm trying to figure out if I should be alarmed," I said. "After all, there is a murderer out there somewhere."

"That's why we're trying to find the killer," he said.

A million dazzling stars danced in the black sky. Crickets chirped in the nearby trees. This brought back memories of the night I'd walked over here and found Evan.

"Are you okay?" Detective Meyer asked.

He must have sensed my uneasiness.

"I just thought about that night," I said.

"If this is too much for you, we can turn around." He gestured over his shoulder.

"No, I'm fine," I said with a wave of my hand.

I didn't want to appear weak. I had to go through with this. The moonlight bounced off the shiny silver parts of Evan's trailer as it came into view and my anxiety increased. Maybe I wasn't ready for this after all. No, I had to push through. A slight breeze rustled the nearby tree branches and I jumped. Yes, I was a bit skittish.

Detective Meyer grabbed me as if he thought I may fall. "It's all right. That was just the wind."

I hated to admit I felt safer with his arms around me. He realized I was looking at his arms around me, so he quickly moved.

"I was a little on edge," I said with a smile.

"That's understandable," he said.

We stepped in front of the trailer. I wasn't sure what would happen to it now. Once the fair was over, I assumed the fair would move. I wasn't sure if Evan had been single, married, or divorced.

"So you said when you came around the side of the trailer you bumped into Caleb?" Detective Meyer asked.

I pushed the hair out of my eyes. "Yes, that's right. I'm not sure which direction he came from."

"You can't say for sure he wasn't already here?"

"It was kind of like he popped up out of nowhere," I said.

"Did he say why he was here to see Evan?" the detective asked.

"Didn't you ask him that?" I asked in return.

"Yes, but I was curious if he gave you the same answer."

"Well, he said he was upset with Evan and wanted to discuss issues with the fair. Are you going to arrest him?" I asked.

The detective peered into the darkness. "We don't have evidence for that."

Was this just a ruse to get me here and ask me questions about why I'd been at the trailer? A pair of handcuffs was attached to the back of his pants. A flash of him placing me under arrest darted through my mind.

"Are you going to arrest me?" My voice wavered. I hadn't planned on asking that. It just sort of came out.

He turned to face me. "Should I?"

"No way." I stuffed my hands in my pockets in case he wanted to handcuff me. "The thought occurred to me that if you're suspicious of Caleb, you might be suspicious of me too."

The thought made my stomach turn.

"Don't worry, Ms. Cabot."

That was easy for him to say. He hadn't specifically said he wouldn't arrest me. Just for me not to worry.

"You can call me Celeste," I said.

He studied my face. "All right, Celeste. As long as you remember to call me Pierce."

A faint smile crossed his lips. That was the only time I'd seen him smile other than when petting Van.

"I'll walk you back to your trailer, Celeste," Pierce said.

As we walked back toward the path, he said, "I thought I heard you talking to someone in your trailer tonight."

"I was talking with Van."

At least Van couldn't tattle on me and deny that.

"It sounded like a lengthy conversation," he said.

"Did you think I was hiding someone in my trailer?" I asked.

"Oh no, I just assumed it was your little dog."

I didn't believe him.

We reached the trailer.

"Thank you for going back to the scene with me. I know it can't be easy for you."

"You're welcome," I said. "I want to help any way I can to find the killer."

Pierce looked at my trailer. "I like your home. Do you live in it full time?"

"Actually, I'm from Gatlinburg."

"Really?" he asked.

Pierce didn't sound that surprised. He was probably just pretending. I suspected he'd checked into my background after the murder.

"It was just easier for me to bring the trailer than driving back and forth to set up each day. I plan on traveling around the region to craft fairs with my Shasta."

"Sounds like you're having a lot of fun. Well, other than the discovery of a murder victim." He grimaced after his comment.

"Yes, that did change things a bit," I said.

I peeked around to see if I spotted Elizabeth. I was curious to see if she was back in the trailer waiting for me. A slight mist traveled around the side of the trailer. Had that been her?

"Well, have a nice evening," Pierce said.

I opened the door and stepped inside. He watched me until I closed the door. Elizabeth was nowhere in sight. I expected her to show up again soon. I never knew when she might pop up.

I peeked out the window to see if the detective was still around. He had gone, but I caught movement out of the corner of my eye. A woman stepped out from the shadows. She'd been standing behind a large oak tree. What was she doing back there? Was she looking in the direction of my trailer? I sensed she may have been watching me. Had she seen me talking with Pierce?

Darkness concealed the woman's identity. After a couple of seconds, she stepped out onto the path. Light from the moon gave me a better look at her face. It was Shar, the jewelry vendor. Why had she been here? She looked in my direction, so

I stepped to the side. Could she see me watching her?

What if she was the killer? What if she was coming for me next? I had to know what she was doing now. I eased back to the window for a peek. Shar was nowhere in sight. Whew. Thank goodness. Maybe she had gone back to her trailer. I released a deep breath and tried to calm my nerves.

There was no way I was going out there to ask her what she was doing. Maybe she was the one sneaking around and stealing people's money. I should call Pierce to let him know. But what if she was just out for an innocent walk? Though I didn't think people hid behind trees when they were out for an evening stroll. Checking out the little window, I looked to the left and to the right. Where had she gone to so quickly?

A knock sounded on the door and I screamed. Van started barking again. There was no way to pretend I wasn't here. Everyone at the fair probably had heard my scream. I reached down and picked up Van and eased the door open to find Ruth on my doorstep.

"Good evening, Ruth."

She eyed me up and down. Obviously, she was upset about something. Her plain white T-shirt had a smudge of what appeared to be mud on the front. Her long, gauzy, light blue skirt had the same stains. She wore the same muddy tennis shoes.

"Were you just messing around my trailer?" she asked.

"No, I've been in here," I said.

She studied my face as if trying to gauge if I was being truthful.

"I thought I saw you." She crossed her arms in front of her waist.

"Maybe it was Shar. I just saw her. Did someone knock on your door?"

She narrowed her eyes. "No, but someone twisted the doorknob. When I went to the window to look out, I just caught a glimpse as the person moved around the side of my trailer. I thought the person walked in this direction. That's why I thought it was you."

"I would never try your door without knocking," I said.

If it was Shar, why did she turn back toward my trailer? Her booth was in the opposite direction. Van growled. Was he growling at Ruth or someone else?

"If I see someone around my trailer again, I'll let them have it," Ruth said through gritted teeth.

She marched back toward her trailer. I peered around to see if I spotted Shar, but nothing seemed unusual. It had to be her, though. Why had she tried Ruth's door? Maybe it was Ruth's imagination. Still, I'd better share this information with Pierce. Van growled again.

"It's okay. She's gone now."

He continued with the sound. Ruth had gone back into her trailer.

"What are you growling at?"

An uneasiness came over me. Stepping back inside, I locked the door. "We're safe now."

I moved back over to the window for one more look. It was eerily quiet out there now. At least Van wasn't growling anymore. Someone had been around. I had a feeling Shar had been lurking.

I picked up my phone. Should I call Pierce now or wait until morning? I hated to call after I'd seen him just a short time earlier. I set the phone back down. It could wait until morning.

What if Shar had been looking for a trailer to break into to steal money? It had been a long day. I should just try to rest and address this in the morning.

CHAPTER 11

Travel trailer tip 11:
Make the space like home by adding things like cozy
lights, pictures, and quilts. If you feel cramped, put up
a poster of a window into a beautiful scene. A pretend
window is better than no window at all.

The sun bathed the morning in warmth. I decided to take Van for a walk to a nearby café. He
could get exercise and I could get a pastry, though
he was so tiny, he usually tired out on walks and I
had to carry him. Having Van snuggled in my arms
was my favorite thing on earth. At night he liked to
curl up next to my head to sleep. One of the sweetest sounds was his breathing in my ear.

Not far from the fair was a stretch of little shops,
a café, and a coffee shop. The coffee shop had the
best croissants I'd ever eaten. Luckily, they had outside seating, so that Van and I could enjoy breakfast
outside in the beautiful weather.

Dressed in my knee-length white shorts, a pink
T-shirt, and sneakers, I headed down the sidewalk
with Van on the leash trotting along beside me. He

stopped several times to sniff various items along our path. Traffic was light because it was early morning. A few people walked up and down the sidewalk, but things were quiet.

Soon we reached the little café. White tables and chairs sat along the patio area out front. A couple of tables were occupied, but Van and I had our pick of the others. I wanted to sit closer to the building so Van wouldn't be tempted to bark at people as they walked by. Well, he'd still bark if he saw them, but he wouldn't be within reach to bite.

Van sat on the chair next to mine as if he was ready to order from the menu. The waitress brought a glass of water for me and some water for Van as well. I had a dish for him that I carried in my tote bag. A breeze drifted across the morning air as I enjoyed my croissant, fruit, and latte. Van was waiting for a bite.

"This is the life, isn't it, Van?" I asked as I gave him a piece of my banana.

A few people had sat down at the table behind us. I hadn't seen them come up because they'd entered from the other side.

"He really made a mess of everything," the man said.

Van was interested in the people at the table, but I couldn't turn around to look without being obvious. The man's voice sounded familiar. I had to peek over my shoulder. I dropped my napkin onto the ground and reached down to pick it up.

As I grabbed the napkin, I looked to the left for a glimpse at the people sitting behind me. I recognized the man. It was Max, who'd taken over for

Evan as the craft fair organizer. Was he talking about Evan? He didn't notice me looking at him. I turned back around and continued to listen to their conversation. I didn't recognize the women with him.

"They're lucky they had me to step in and run the thing. I plan on doing a lot with the craft show. As you know, I'll be taking over for Evan at the museum too."

He sure did talk a lot. And it seemed as if all the talk was strictly about him.

"Do they have any leads on who killed him?" one of the women asked.

"Not that I'm aware of. Did I tell you that I have a new project I'll be doing at the museum?"

Wow. He had immediately switched the conversation back to himself. He didn't seem interested in the least if the police found Evan's killer. Maybe that was because he already knew who had killed Evan.

When my phone rang, I almost jumped out of my chair. I snatched the phone so that it would stop ringing. I didn't want to draw attention to myself. I would have sent the call to voice mail but Mom's face was splashed across the screen. It was the picture of her next to the Dolly Parton statue outside of the Sevier County courthouse. My mother wanted to have her picture taken with Dolly Parton, but until that happened, the bronze statue would have to do.

"Hello," I whispered.

My mother paused. "Celeste, what's wrong? Have you lost your voice?"

Just as I was ready to tell her that I'd call her back, Max and his dining guests stood from the table.

"Hold on just a minute, Mom," I said.

Max and the women walked by my table. He didn't even glance my way. Van refrained from barking at them. It was as if he knew I was trying to go unnoticed. As they walked down the sidewalk away from the café, I assumed they were headed back to the fairgrounds.

"Okay, I'm back," I said.

"Where are you?" she asked.

"I'm at a café. I just overheard the man who took over operations of the fair talking about what a mess Evan made of everything."

"He said that?" my mother asked.

"Yes. His name is Max. He thinks it's a good thing he's here to take over, now that Evan is gone."

"Do you think he got rid of Evan so he could take over?" my mother asked.

"That doesn't sound like a reason to murder someone," I said.

"Some people really don't need an excuse. Sociopaths will find the slightest thing to use as their reason. Is he gone now?"

I released a deep breath. "Yes, thank goodness. I'm going to finish my breakfast and head back to the fairgrounds."

"Just be careful," my mother said. "I worry about you."

"Don't worry about me. I'll be fine."

After ending the call, I finished the croissant so that I could hurry back to the fairgrounds. I wanted to find out more about Max. Who was he and where had he worked before coming to the craft fair?

Instead of walking Van with his leash, I carried him so that I could get back to the fairgrounds quicker. I had no idea where to start in my quest for more info about Max. I supposed I should find out who the women were. Maybe I could ask them questions about Max, though they probably wouldn't give details to a stranger.

After a short walk, Van and I arrived back at the fair. Now I had to track down Max. He was staying in a small white trailer by the office. He probably wondered why his trailer wasn't as big as the one they'd let Evan use while running the craft fair. His was half the size of the one Evan had, and not nearly as fancy-looking. If he wasn't there, I would have to find out where he'd gone. I didn't even know for sure he was going back to the fair once he left the café. I put Van back in my trailer so he could take a nap. It had been an eventful morning for him, and I knew he liked to sleep in the mid-morning.

Customers would be arriving soon. If I hurried, I could stop by Max's and, with any luck, track down the women he'd been dining with this morning. After that, I'd rush back over to my trailer and put out my paintings. Every time I thought of my paintings now, I thought about Elizabeth. I wondered if she'd make another appearance or if she was gone for good.

Because it was Saturday, the office was closed. It only opened Monday through Friday. I had the rest of today and tomorrow and the fair would be over. The small trailer next to the office had been

where Max said he was staying. Tall oak trees surrounded the little trailer. Should I knock on the
door? I paused, standing by one of the trees. Maybe
I'd just watch for a few seconds and see what happened. No one was around.

Just as I was getting up my nerve to walk up to
the trailer to knock, the women stepped out. They
waved at Max and headed down the path away
from the trailer. I had to make a decision. Should I
talk with Max or follow the women?

I decided to follow the women. Max would always be there, but I might never see the women
again. I hurried away from the trailer and fell in
behind them. Both were lithe, as if maybe they
were marathon runners. Could they be sisters?
They had the same shade of ash-brown hair cut in
similar, shoulder-length styles. One was a couple of
inches taller than the other. The women wore
shorts showing their muscular legs, sneakers, and
casual shirts designed to keep cool on summer
days like this one. So far, they didn't act as if they
knew I was following them. I had no idea how I
would start a conversation. They would think I was
strange if I just started talking to them.

I picked up my pace so I could catch up with
them. If I walked beside them, I could start a conversation. I wanted to know who they were and
how they knew Max. The women were chatting,
but I couldn't make out what they were saying. I
hated to interrupt, but with each passing second, I
was missing an opportunity to uncover information that might lead to solving this murder. I was
now walking right beside them. Looking over at

them would be too obvious, so I tried to act casual, as if I was just out for a stroll.

"Do you think we should still talk to him?" the woman next to me asked the other.

Were they discussing Max? I should listen to the conversation as long as possible—until they noticed me.

"Betsy, how are you?" I called out in a loud voice.

The women looked at me with frowns on their faces.

"I'm sorry?" the one closest to me said.

"Oh, forgive me, I thought you were a friend named Betsy."

She smiled. "No, my name isn't Betsy."

"Are you a vendor here?" I asked as we continued walking.

"Actually, no, we're just here looking around the fair."

"Oh, how nice. There are a lot of great things."

They studied me for a second, and then the woman said, "Are *you* a vendor here?"

I smiled. "Yes, I have paintings at my booth right up there."

The woman looked in the direction of my pointing finger.

"We'd love to see your work," the other woman said.

I thought they were just being nice. That worked out fine for me, though. This would give me an opportunity to talk with them more about Max.

"I can show you. Just follow me."

We headed toward my booth.

"I think we saw you earlier at the café," the woman said.

"Oh really? Yes, I was there. I don't recall seeing you." I wondered if my acting was believable.

"You had that adorable little chihuahua," she said.

I chuckled. "Yes, he's taking a nap right now. It's a nice café. Do you eat there often?"

We had reached my booth now, though I didn't have any of the paintings out yet.

"We just stopped by there this morning with a friend from work. You probably know him," the woman said.

"Oh really?" I asked, trying to sound casual.

"His name is Max. He's the director of this fair."

"Well, he is now," the other woman said.

"Yes, I know him."

"It's tragic what happened."

"Yes, it is. Max is probably upset about it," I said.

I knew the answer to that already and hoped the women would confirm it. They exchanged a look. That was all I needed.

"He is probably still in shock," the woman said.

"Does he have any idea who killed Evan?" I asked. "Maybe he mentioned something."

"He was too busy talking about being the director now."

The other woman shook her head at her friend.

"What? It's the truth. He was acting so strange. It was rather upsetting."

I tried to act shocked by her admission, but I wasn't in the least. I'd seen Max's behavior.

"Do you think he had anything to do with Evan's death?" I asked.

I wasn't sure how they would react to my question.

"Oh, I don't know. That sounds extreme. Surely he wouldn't have done anything like that."

"I don't know. He was acting strange," the woman repeated.

I took the paintings out from the storage container as I listened to her. I had to ask more about Max.

"You said you work with Max. Where is that?" I hardly knew anything about Max.

The women stepped closer to look at my paintings. "These are lovely," the taller woman said, gesturing at the canvas with a lake and geese in flight. "Your paintings have so much personality."

"Thank you," I said with a smile.

"He's always been a very driven person, like he wants to succeed at all costs. No matter who he had to push out of the way or step on in order to get there."

"Are you friends with him?" I asked.

"I suppose you could say we're on friendly terms."

"He never tried to step on you or push you out of the way?"

"We weren't trying for the same position, but if we had been, he probably would have."

"And you like being friends with someone like that?" I asked.

"It never really came up. Until recently, when it got worse." She checked her watch, and I wondered if that was a hint that she needed to leave.

"I suppose I understand," I said.

All I really learned from this conversation was

what I kind of knew in the first place. Max was cut-throat, so I could see where he could possibly be the murderer, However, I didn't have definitive proof, which was what I was looking for.

As I brought out the paintings, I paused with my hands on Elizabeth's portrait. I wasn't sure what to do with it. What if someone wanted to buy it? Could I sell them the painting with a ghost attached? Regardless, I placed it next to the others. I was on edge waiting for the ghost to pop back up again.

"What a lovely painting," one of the women said as she focused on the canvas of Elizabeth.

Now I was regretting bringing out that portrait. I should've left it in storage and out of view.

"You know, it looks like the woman who lived in that mansion across town."

"Oh, the one that's on the historic register?" the other woman asked.

"Yes, that's the one. Is that where you got the inspiration for the painting?" she asked.

CHAPTER 12

Travel trailer tip 12:
Prep meals at home before you set out in your trailer. It'll
save time and require less cleanup. Plus, you'll be less
likely to feel the urge to indulge in kettle corn.

That evening, after a full day of customers, I decided to take Van for a walk around the craft fair. I attached the leash to his collar and set off down the path. Van would probably insist I carry him back. His little legs only went so far before getting tired.

The evening breeze carried across the wind, caressing my arms and shoulders. The heat was still hanging on, but it was slightly cooler today than yesterday. Streaks of red and blue filled the sky as the sun quickly made its descent. I figured I'd better finish up the walk soon. After all, there was still an unsolved murder. Nighttime would give the murderer plenty of places to hide. I didn't want to be the next victim.

I hadn't spoken to Caleb since our dinner date. I'd missed his call and he hadn't left a message. I was torn on whether I should call him back. I figured I would see him around, but so far, I hadn't. I just so happened to be walking in the direction of his booth. Not on purpose. Okay, it was on purpose.

Butterflies danced in my stomach as I neared his booth. I had no idea why. I didn't see him anywhere. I caught movement and noticed a woman by his booth. It was Shar. I'd recognize her bright hair peeking out from that baseball cap anywhere. She turned and looked in my direction.

I stepped out of the way and hid behind an adjacent trailer, pressing my body against the white-metal exterior. I hoped its occupants didn't see me lurking around and think I was the thief or the murderer. Shar didn't act as if she'd seen me. I recognized her, though. Why was she messing around Caleb's trailer? She'd been spying on me the night of Evan's murder too. Plus, Ruth said someone had tried to open her door.

Was Shar the one who was stealing money? What other reason would she have for snooping around? What if she was the killer too? Now panic hit me. What if she was looking for Caleb to off him too? What would be her motive? I knew she'd been mad at Evan, but was she angry with Caleb as well?

"What do you think she's doing?" a woman asked from over my shoulder.

As I jumped, Van barked.

Elizabeth stood next to me. "Oh, did I scare you, Ms. Celeste? I'm sorry."

"Yes, just a little," I said as I picked up Van.

"I saw you watching that woman." Elizabeth pointed to Shar.

"She's been snooping around trailers. I think she might be stealing from the vendors," I whispered.

"That's not a nice thing to do," Elizabeth said. "You should tell the detective."

"Yes, I probably should," I said.

"Of course, you've been snooping around too." Elizabeth watched Shar.

"Totally necessary," I said.

We stood in silence as we waited for Shar to make her move. If she acted as if she was going into Caleb's trailer, I would call 911.

"Should I go confront her?" I asked.

"It could be dangerous. I think you should wait for the police to handle it," Elizabeth said.

Unfortunately, if Shar did something, I might not have a choice but to confront her. I couldn't let her do anything to Caleb. There would be no time to wait for the police to arrive. Shar proceeded toward Caleb's trailer. I moved out from behind my hiding spot and inched closer to her. She was by Caleb's door now.

Just as she reached out to wrap her hand around the doorknob, I spotted Caleb coming up the path toward his trailer. Shar noticed him too, because she quickly moved away from the door. He hadn't spotted Shar yet. I knew she would act as if she hadn't been up to something fishy.

Shar took off in the opposite direction. I had to tell Caleb what I'd seen and hope he didn't suspect me of snooping around. Okay, as Elizabeth had pointed out, I had been snooping around, but I didn't want him to think I was doing it.

With Van in my arms, I walked over to Caleb's

booth. At the moment, his artwork wasn't out. It made the space feel empty and lonely. When Caleb spotted me, a smile spread across his face. At least that was a good sign. A killer wouldn't look so nice, would he?

"I didn't expect to see you tonight. I tried to call you. I thought maybe you'd like to go for ice cream." Caleb reached out and rubbed Van's head, and Van immediately licked Caleb's hand. "I bet Van would like ice cream too."

I chuckled. "Van likes everything. Except broccoli. He's not a fan."

Caleb nodded. "I don't blame you for that, Van."

"What about Gum Shoe? Would he like ice cream too?"

"He hasn't mastered the art of dining in public. He's still technically a puppy," Caleb said.

"Oh, it's tough. Especially when ice cream is involved," I said. "Actually, the reason I'm here was because I just spotted Shar at your trailer. I don't know that she was here for a friendly visit."

"What makes you say that?" Caleb asked.

"I think she was trying to get in your trailer."

"Maybe she was just at the door knocking."

"I suppose that could have been the case." Honestly, it hadn't looked that way to me.

"I can ask her if she needed something," Caleb said.

"I saw her at Ruth's trailer too. Well, I didn't see her there, but Ruth saw her. I also noticed her watching my place."

"Have you shared this with the police?" Caleb asked.

"Not yet. I probably should, though," I said.

He studied my face. "You look stressed. What do you say about the ice cream?"

"Stressed" was one way to put it. Ice cream wouldn't do the trick to get rid of the nervousness either. Plus, I couldn't just let my suspicions of Caleb go that easily.

"Come on." He motioned. "The ice cream place is just down the way."

It was a close walk. And it wasn't quite dark yet, although it would be soon.

I nodded. "Okay. Ice cream is good."

We moved down the path toward the main street that led into the fairgrounds.

"Do you think Shar was trying to get into your trailer to look for money?" I asked.

"It's possible," Caleb said. "This trip for ice cream is meant to help you destress, though. Talking about the crime probably won't make that happen."

"I guess you're right."

Soon, we reached the sidewalk and traveled the short distance to the ice cream shop. A pink neon sign flashed the name Scoops.

"I doubt they'll let Van in the shop," I said as I cradled him in my arms.

"It's okay, I'll go in and order for us," Caleb said. "What kind of ice cream would you like?"

I peered in at the chalkboard menu on the wall. With so many options, it was a tough decision, but I went with my usual.

"My favorite is cookies 'n cream," I said.

"Sugar cone or waffle?" Caleb gestured.

"Sugar cone."

"No hesitation with that decision," Caleb said around a chuckle. "Okay, I'll be back in a jiffy."

When Caleb opened the door, a blast of cold air swooshed out onto the sidewalk. The whirl of a blender echoed from inside. He stepped inside, leaving Van and me alone on the sidewalk. Traffic was light, but a few cars still traveled down the street in front of the shop. No doubt the heat would melt our ice cream quickly. We'd have to lick fast. Van and I sat at one of the little iron tables out front. I watched the moving cars and a few people as they passed by, walking to different locations. Van seemed entertained by the action too.

A couple of minutes later, Caleb joined us. He handed me a towering ice cream cone, stacked high with three scoops of white creamy goodness sprinkled with chunks of cookie. If I wasn't careful, the weight of the ice cream would tip the small cone right over.

"Thank you," I said with wide eyes as I wondered how I'd make even a dent in the dessert.

"You're welcome." Caleb took the seat next to me at the table and proceeded to dig into a banana split towering with whipped cream.

Van watched us intently as we ate the treats. After discussing our art and the fair for a bit, I shifted the conversation back to the murder. I couldn't help myself.

"Have you spoken with the detective again?" I asked.

Caleb shifted in his seat. "Yes, he's been around a few times. I've told him everything I know. What about you?"

I took another lick of the ice cream. "Same here."

"I suppose they think I may have had something to do with the murder," Caleb said as he savored his bite.

I was surprised he had mentioned this.

"I'm not sure," I said. "Just because you were there doesn't mean you had anything to do with it. I was there too, so I suppose people think the same of me."

The thought of finding Caleb at the scene had crossed my mind a lot. The police had to think the same. Which meant the police had me on their list of suspects too.

"You have a bit of ice cream on your nose." I pointed at Caleb.

He touched his nose with a napkin. "It's good stuff, huh?"

I chuckled. "Too good, apparently."

"What about you, Celeste? Do you think I murdered Evan?" Caleb finished his ice cream, saving the cherry for last.

Never did I think I'd be asked that question over a scoop of frozen dessert. I couldn't say yes. This was one time I would have to lie.

"No, of course not," I said, trying to sound casual.

I wasn't sure how well I had pulled it off. He stared at me, and my anxiety spiked. I had to turn this around. "What about you? Do you think I murdered Evan?"

"It's true, you were there," he said.

Oh no. Why was he having ice cream with me if he suspected me of such a horrendous thing?

"No, I don't think you would ever do something like that. So if that rules us out, who do you think did it?"

Whew. I hoped he was being truthful. My brothers were already giving me a hard time about being a murderer. I didn't like for people to think badly of me.

"What about Shar? She's been sneaking around trailers. Plus, she was mad at Evan that night."

Caleb leaned back in the chair. "I honestly don't know. It sounds as if you've been thinking about this quite a bit, though."

I wiped my mouth with a napkin. "It has been on my mind quite a bit."

That wasn't the only thing on my mind either. I wanted to tell someone about Elizabeth, but the last thing I wanted was for everyone to think I was crazy. It would sound completely insane if I said the person from my painting had come to life. Well, not exactly to life, but had been animated. I'd brought a spirit out of my artwork.

"Do you have any other suspects in mind?" Caleb asked, breaking my thoughts.

I cradled Van in my arms. He had given up on the ice cream now that it was gone and was napping in my arms.

"Well, there were a few people unhappy with Evan. It could even be my neighbor, Ruth," I said.

Caleb chuckled. "That cute little old lady?"

"She would be the last person you would suspect, right? That's what would make it the perfect crime. She could get away with it because no one would suspect her."

"No, you're right, they wouldn't suspect her," Caleb said.

"You know, I get a strange vibe from Ruth. When we first met, she seemed nice, but things changed as soon as the murder occurred."

"Do you think she suspects you of being the killer?"

"I think maybe that's the case. Plus, I've seen her snooping around." I paused as Caleb studied my face. "I've often wondered if she was the one taking the money."

"Have you shared this with the detective?" he asked.

"I've just been trying to handle it on my own. I suppose I've been playing detective."

"That's a bit dangerous. Maybe you should leave that to the police," Caleb said.

Why was I telling Caleb all this? No way would I tell him that I had my own suspects list. I was being an amateur sleuth. If he was the killer, he would want to get rid of me. Furthermore, why had I walked to the ice cream shop with him?

"I suppose I should just keep an eye on her," I said.

"Well, be careful. I really think you should tell the detective about this."

Why was he pressing for me to tell the detective? Unless he wanted the detective off his trail. Our talking seemed so casual and came so easily, I really hoped Caleb wasn't the murderer.

"You never told me about your other job," I said.

This was for Aunt Patsy. She had made me curious.

"Did I say I had another job?" he asked. "Maybe you just misunderstood me. Wood sculpting is what I do full time."

He seemed a bit uneasy about my question. This was more suspicious behavior.

We sat in silence. I knew Caleb was thinking about what I'd said.

After a few more seconds, I said, "Well, I suppose I should get Van to bed. He's tired."

Caleb smiled. "Yes, I see he's ready for bedtime."

Caleb and I walked back to the fairgrounds. It was a pleasant walk and we discussed our art again, plus our plans after this fair was over. There was another fair he was going to in a couple of weeks and I had thought about going as well. Several times, I thought about telling him about the ghost, but I stopped myself. I wanted to tell someone so badly, but I didn't know of anyone who would believe me. As wacky as my parents were, even they probably wouldn't believe me if I told them. This was something I would have to keep to myself.

We'd just turned a corner and my trailer was in sight when I spotted movement up ahead. There was definitely someone outside the trailer. Caleb must've noticed it at the exact same time.

"Who is that?" he asked.

"I don't know, but I don't think they should be around my trailer."

Immediately, Shar came to mind, but I wasn't sure if it was her. It was too dark and the person was still too far away for me to be certain. I was almost sure it was a woman. I figured it was a safe assumption to think it was Shar because I'd seen her at Caleb's trailer. She had to be the person breaking in and stealing money.

Caleb ran over toward my trailer. I supposed he wanted to catch her in the act. I hurried as well, but I was holding Van in my arms, so I couldn't run as fast. I didn't want to fall. Plus, I wasn't really prepared to confront anyone. What if she was the killer? Now I was worried about Caleb. And yet I had suspected he was the murderer. I was so confused because the clues were leading me in many different directions.

Caleb reached my trailer and went out of sight around the side. For all I knew, she could've been waiting for him as soon as he turned that corner. My anxiety spiked.

As soon as I reached the trailer, Caleb popped up in front of me. I jumped and Van barked until he realized who it was.

"Are you all right?" I asked.

"Whoever it was, I didn't catch them. They were gone quickly, but it was a woman."

"Do you think it was Shar?" I asked.

He released a deep breath. "There's just no way for me to know for sure. I only saw the back of the person and it was dark. She was dressed in black."

"Like a cat burglar or a murderer," I said.

"We should call the police and report this," Caleb said.

I nodded. "Yes, you're right. Let me put Van inside the trailer and I'll place the call."

Once Van was secure in the Shasta with his food, water, and bed, I joined Caleb outside again. I pulled out my phone and also the detective's card, so that I could call his number directly. He picked up, and I told him what had happened.

"Maybe you should've just called 911," Caleb said.

"I'm not sure this is exactly an emergency right now, and the detective is working the case, so I figured I could just give him a call."

"I guess." Caleb shoved his hands into his pockets.

I got the feeling Caleb didn't like the detective much. I supposed he felt being a suspect was reason enough not to call the detective. Being a suspect myself, I understood why he felt that way.

I was amazed at how many police officers showed up within a matter of minutes. Pierce made eye contact with me right away as he walked over to my trailer.

"I had no idea so many police would show up," I said.

"Well, this is an active crime investigation and there's a lot going on here," he said, glancing over at Caleb. "Tell me what happened."

An undeniable tension hung in the air between them. I supposed some people just instantly took a dislike for others.

"Caleb and I went out for ice cream."

Pierce's gaze traveled over to Caleb again. Why did I feel odd telling the detective about this? Pierce had a strange look on his face. I did find him attractive, but he hadn't asked me out for ice cream. Caleb had. Though Caleb could be a murderer, for heaven's sake.

"And what happened?" Pierce asked.

"We just came back and saw someone around my trailer. But that wasn't all. Earlier in the evening, when I went to Caleb's booth, I noticed someone around his trailer as well."

"You went to Caleb's booth?" Pierce cast a skeptical eye my way.

"Yes," I said.

Pierce exchanged a look with Caleb before turning his attention back to me. "Do you think it was the same person?"

"I don't know if it's the same person, but I saw Shar at Caleb's. You spoke with her before."

"I'll make sure to speak with her again," he said. "Was your trailer still secure?"

"Yes, the door was locked," I said.

Movement caught my attention. Elizabeth stood by the edge of the trailer. She waved enthusiastically. Detective Meyer noticed I was watching something.

"Is everything okay, Celeste, um, Ms. Cabot?" he asked.

Elizabeth waved again. It looked as if she wanted to speak with me. Maybe she'd gotten a look at the woman we'd seen. Even if she had seen the snoop, I couldn't share that information with the detective. I couldn't tell Pierce my source was a ghost. That would be the same as if I said Van told me. He'd think I'd lost my marbles. I was curious to hear what Elizabeth had to say, though.

What if I spoke with Shar? Maybe she'd admit she was snooping around. Whatever Elizabeth told me, I would use that information and investigate on my own. There would be no harm in that. I pulled my attention away from Elizabeth and focused on Pierce again.

"Did you notice anything else?" Pierce asked.

"Not that I can recall. Well, other than that Shar has been snooping around other trailers. I saw her watching mine last night."

"And you didn't tell me about that sooner?" Pierce looked to Caleb. "Did you know about this?"

Caleb didn't answer.

"I planned on telling you," I said, feeling a bit as if I'd been scolded by my parents.

"Please, if anything else happens, tell me right away. Even if it's minor," Pierce said.

I nodded. "I will."

Pierce looked at Caleb. "I'll be in touch soon."

He walked away from us. It looked as if he was headed in the direction of Shar's.

"He seems unhappy," Caleb said.

"That's a bad thing," I said.

"Don't worry about him. He's just doing his job." Caleb offered a smile that under less stressful circumstances would make me melt.

I had a feeling I'd made Pierce a bit angry with me. I hadn't meant to keep the information from him. It just worked out that way. At least now the activity had settled down. The police hadn't found any sign of the intruder. For the rest of the evening, I'd worry about the woman coming back.

Later that night, after the police had gone and all was quiet, Van slept and I cozied up with a book. Of course I was on edge, waiting for either the killer or Elizabeth to show up. Of the two, I'd much prefer to see Elizabeth.

When my phone rang, I nearly jumped out of my chair. My best friend's picture appeared on the phone's screen. I was sure she wondered what in the world was going on over here, because I'd left her a bit of a panicked voice mail. There wasn't much we didn't know about each other, though Sammie soon might discover something new about me.

"For heaven's sake, Celeste, you had me scared nearly to death. What's happened now?" Sammie asked.

With a bit of frantic rambling, I explained what had happened.

"Maybe it's time you pulled out of that craft fair," she said.

"That would be the wise decision, but it's so close to the end now. Plus, I really want to sell more of my art."

"The end could be more than you think if you don't get out of there."

I wanted to tell her about the other thing on my mind. What was I worried about? If anyone would understand it would be Sammie.

"There was one other thing I wanted to tell you."

"I knew there was something else going on. Is it about the detective or Caleb?" Sammie asked.

"Neither," I said.

"Bummer," she said.

"Well, here goes . . . I think I've seen a ghost."

There was a pause. Sammie knew I had never believed in ghosts.

"Okay," she said. "Where did you see this ghost?"

At least she was willing to hear me out. I knew she would try to offer a logical explanation. Sammie was a logical person.

The story flowed from my lips. It felt great just to get all of it off my mind. To finally release the story that I'd been keeping to myself. Van hadn't offered feedback, so I needed a human to help me decide what to do.

"You have been under a lot of stress since the discovery of the body," Sammie said.

"Yes, but that doesn't explain the other woman saying the painting is haunted."

"Maybe once she said it, that made you susceptible to experiencing it as well. After all, you do have a vivid imagination. It's just part of being artistic."

I knew she'd try to be logical about this, but I didn't want to hear that she thought this was all in my head. If only she would see Elizabeth too. Then she'd believe me.

"Maybe we should go out tomorrow. How about shopping? Lunch or the movies?" Sammie asked.

"I have to be here tomorrow," I said.

She groaned. "You mean you're staying?"

"Sammie, you should know I always finish what I start," I said.

"You shouldn't finish what you start when that something is bad for you," she said.

"I'll be fine," I said.

"I'm coming over there tomorrow. I should have been there sooner."

"You had to pick up that fantastic antique table you found at the estate sale in Knoxville. I understand. I'm always amazed at your ability to find such stunning pieces."

"Well, tomorrow is my day off. I'll see you then. In the meantime, please be careful. And try not to stress out too much."

CHAPTER 13

Travel trailer tip 13:
Pack a first aid kit. Life inside a trailer can be
hazardous. So can life outside a trailer.

The sun streamed through the tree branches, casting a prism of colors across the front of my trailer. I surveyed the setup of my paintings.

"Looks good," a baritone voice said from over my shoulder.

I spun around to find Caleb standing right behind me. It was a bit disconcerting that I hadn't heard him when he slipped up.

"Oh, thank you," I said with a smile.

He studied my work for a bit longer. No matter how many paintings I sold, I always felt self-conscious when people looked at my work. What was he thinking? Did he hate them? The portrait of Elizabeth was there, but I knew I wouldn't sell her now.

"I want to buy one of your paintings," Caleb said.

I almost asked why, but that would be an odd question to ask of a customer. If he wanted to buy,

I certainly couldn't refuse. Maybe he liked my work after all.

"Okay," I said hesitantly. "Which one would you like?"

He stepped closer, studying the paintings again. I walked along beside him with butterflies in my stomach.

"Which one do you like best?" he asked.

"Well, I'm sure you know that's like asking a mother to pick her favorite child."

He chuckled. "Yes, I suppose it is."

He stopped in front of the painting of Elizabeth. Oh no. I knew I should have removed it. I'd have to tell him it wasn't for sale. After that, he'd want to know why. It would turn into a whole big thing. I wasn't good at lying.

"What about this one? Do you know this person?" He pointed. "An ancestor?"

Could Elizabeth be an ancestor? I hadn't thought of that. Maybe I should show my grandmother the painting to see if she recognized Elizabeth. Movement caught my attention. Elizabeth peeked around the side of my trailer.

"I'm not exactly sure who she is," I said.

"She's mesmerizing." Caleb turned his attention to me. "Like you."

Heat rushed to my cheeks.

"Why, thank you," Elizabeth said.

I jumped when she spoke. I hadn't realized she'd moved so close to us. Caleb looked at me strangely.

"Yes, it is a unique piece," I said.

"It's almost . . . haunting," Caleb said.

What made him pick *that* word?

"Unfortunately, it's not for sale." I rushed the words.

He frowned. "Why not? Does it have a special meaning for you?"

"You could say that." I shifted from one foot to the other. This whole conversation was making me uncomfortable.

"Now I'm curious. Come on, tell me the whole story." Caleb wiggled his fingers, urging for details.

I supposed I could tell him the first part of the story. Leaving out the fact that I'd seen Elizabeth would be the best way to handle this.

"I sold the painting once. It was returned."

"The customer didn't like it?" he asked.

"She loved it at first. However, when she got it home, she said something happened." I studied his face for a reaction.

He waited to hear the rest.

"She claimed the painting was haunted."

Caleb chuckled. "Was she serious?"

"She said she saw a ghost. It was the woman from the painting."

Caleb shook his head. "She probably just dreamed it. There are crazy people out there."

Yes, crazy people, as in murderers.

"I wish it was that simple," I said.

He furrowed his brow. "What do you mean?"

I was nervous about saying more. But maybe I could tell Caleb about Elizabeth after all. What did I have to lose?

"At first, I didn't believe the woman. I thought she just wanted to return the painting. Which was fine," I said.

"Right," Caleb said. "What happened next?"

My heart sped up. I hoped he didn't think I was crazy for telling him this. It would feel better to tell someone else other than Sammie, though. At least that was what I told myself.

"I saw the ghost too," I blurted out.

He chuckled. When I didn't laugh in return, he stopped. "Are you serious?"

"Do you believe in ghosts?" I asked.

He shoved his hands in his pants pockets. "I never put much thought in it. I suppose it's possible, though."

"Oh, it's definitely possible. As a matter of fact, the ghost is here now. She liked when you gave her a compliment by saying she was mesmerizing."

"The ghost talks to you?" His eyes widened.

"Yes," I said.

Now I was second-guessing whether I should have confided in Caleb.

"What else does she say?" Caleb asked.

I couldn't read whether he truly believed me or not.

"Her name is Elizabeth and she doesn't know why she's here."

"Do you know why she's here?" he asked.

"I think it has something to do with this." I reached over and picked up the jar I used to see the hidden images. "Look at the paintings. All of them. I've painted images into them that I didn't know about."

He regarded me skeptically but ultimately took the jar and peered into the glass at the painting. "Interesting." He moved over to another painting and studied it too. After looking at that canvas, he moved on to another and then another. "All of them have a hidden image?"

I nodded. "All of them."

"And you don't remember painting them?"

"Nope."

"That's fascinating. I would say it's matrixing, but the images are so vivid. Plus, they are all similar, with the same theme. It's like a painting within a painting. You're talented."

"Thanks," I said with a blush. "But I didn't know I was doing it."

"Why do you think this has something to do with the ghost?"

"It's just a feeling. The images have a bit of a paranormal twist to them, don't you think?" I asked.

"Yes, I suppose they do," he said as he handed the jar back to me.

"I'd love to find out why this happened and what it all means."

"Why don't you let me buy the painting to see if the ghost follows me? Is she still here?" Caleb looked over my shoulder.

I scanned the area. "I don't see her now."

I wasn't sure how I felt about his proposal. However, what was the worst that could happen? Maybe Elizabeth would be mad at me for selling her to someone else. She would mess up Caleb's stuff like the other woman said had happened to her.

Caleb watched me for an answer.

"I can do that."

"Great. How much do you want for it?" He pulled out his wallet.

He took out a wad of cash. Wow, that was a lot of money. I didn't realize he'd sold so many of his sculptures.

I held up my hand. "You know, I'd rather not sell the painting. I could let you borrow it for a bit instead. Just to see if the ghost comes around."

He put the cash back into his wallet. "I understand."

Elizabeth was back with a scowl on her face. "I don't want to go with him. I want to stay with you. You're the one who painted me. It's meant for me to stay with you. Why do you think I threw such a fit when the other person took me home?" Elizabeth asked from over my shoulder.

I didn't know what to do.

"Are you all right?" Caleb asked.

"The ghost is talking," I said, motioning over my shoulder.

"What is she saying?" Caleb looked around for Elizabeth.

"She doesn't want to go with you."

"Oh, I see," he said with a hint of disappointment in his voice.

Now he thought I was just making it up so he wouldn't take the painting.

"But that's okay. It's important that you take it." I reached over and picked up the canvas.

"Are you sure?" Caleb asked as he took the painting from me.

I nodded. "I'm positive."

When I checked over my shoulder, Elizabeth wasn't back there. I'd probably made her mad. That might be a good thing, though. Now maybe she'd act up, and Caleb would know I was telling the truth. My mind went back to the money in Caleb's wallet.

"Is business good? Have you sold a lot of pieces?" I asked.

He ran his hand through his hair. "Not a lot."

How odd. Did he always keep that much cash on him? Especially with someone at the fair stealing? Was he being honest with me about his career? Just because Caleb was finer than frog hair, it was hard for me to tell him no.

"I promise I'll take good care of it. Elizabeth, you'll be fine with me." Caleb spoke in the direction in which I'd previously pointed out Elizabeth. She'd moved now, though, and stood behind Caleb.

"Thank you," I said.

Caleb picked up the canvas. "Well, I'll get this back to my trailer. I'll let you know if anything happens."

Skepticism filled his voice. With any luck, he would see differently soon. I watched as he walked down the path with the painting. I was oddly attached to it now that Elizabeth had made an appearance. I looked around for her, but she was nowhere in sight.

As I scanned the area, a chill came over me. It wasn't from the weather, and I didn't feel it was from Elizabeth either. It felt as if someone was watching me. With the cover of night, it was a real possibility that someone was hiding nearby. I wouldn't be able to easily spot them. Was it Shar or Carly? The light was on in Ruth's trailer. That didn't mean she was in there, though.

I hurried into my trailer. Van looked up when I entered, but he laid his little head back down and closed his eyes. He was such a sweetheart. The best friend I'd ever had.

After getting ready for bed, I settled down under the covers. Guilt consumed me that I'd given the painting to Caleb when Elizabeth hadn't wanted to go with him. I closed my eyes and tried to sleep, attempting to push the eerie thoughts out of my head.

CHAPTER 14

Travel trailer tip 14:
Keep your belongings locked away securely.
Better yet, leave them at home.

I headed toward the refreshment stand. I needed something sweet to get me going. I'd only made it a few steps from my booth when I fell in behind Carly. She hadn't looked back to know that I was behind her.

A few more steps and she dropped her bag. The contents spilled across the ground. She glanced back and realized I was right there. When our eyes met, a strange look came over her face. I hurried over to help her pick up the contents.

"That's okay," she said with a wave of her hand. "I've got it."

She seemed adamant that I not help her, so I pushed to my feet. Was she trying to hide something? She was shoving items back into her bag at a frantic pace. She had a lot of cash. That wasn't all I noticed either. One of the items I recognized. It was a carving knife that looked a lot like the one

I'd seen sticking out from Evan's neck. Carly didn't sculpt as far as I knew, so why would she have this knife in her bag? I wouldn't just let this discovery go without mentioning it to her.

"I didn't know that you did wood sculpting too," I said.

Carly displayed a fake smile and nervously chuckled. "It's something I just started. I'm not good at it. That's why I haven't told anyone about it."

If this was the truth, why did she seem so nervous? Furthermore, why would she need to carry that knife around with her? It wasn't like she'd do wood carvings on the go.

Carly placed the bag on her shoulder again. "Well, it was nice chatting with you."

She turned and hurried down the path. She shouldn't think she'd get rid of me that easily. As I continued down the path behind her, she peeped over her shoulder.

"I was going this way too," I said with a smile.

She turned her attention back to the path in front of us. I didn't believe her about the wood sculpting. I should have asked to see some of her work. But she would only say no.

I would have to snoop around her booth to see if I noticed anything else. I assumed Carly was headed for the refreshment stand as well. But as we neared the stand, she turned to the left and hurried away. I thought about following her from there, but that would just be strange.

It didn't look as if she was going to her booth. She could be leaving the grounds for all I knew. I could possibly sneak over to her booth while she wasn't there, though she would probably have everything secured in her trailer. What would the detective say about this? I ordered coffee and headed back toward my booth. I would make a slight detour and stop off at Carly's booth first. I hoped she didn't catch me there. I also hoped no one else saw me snooping around her trailer.

I sipped my coffee and tried to act casual, as if nothing was wrong. On the inside, I was nervous. I didn't want Carly to catch me. I felt I had a bit of time, though, because I'd watched her walk in the opposite direction. I hoped no one else spotted me.

As I walked by Shar's booth, I spotted her working with her jewelry. She didn't notice me at first, but when she looked over, our eyes met. I attempted a smile, but she didn't smile in return. She turned her attention back to her work. I hoped she didn't follow me. If she caught me at Carly's, she'd tell her for sure.

When I reached Carly's booth, I looked around to see if anyone was paying attention to me. A few people had looked at me as I walked by, but they weren't watching me now. I stepped over to the booth as if I was just going to cut through to the other side. There was another row of booths behind Carly's.

As I made it to the side of her trailer, I scanned the area for anything suspicious. I wasn't even sure what I should look for. I wanted to see if there were any wood sculptures. Was she telling the truth when she said she was trying her hand at carving? I felt as if it was just her way of explaining the knife. Had she reserved that knife for her next victim?

I had to find that out before she actually went after the person. I had a feeling the killer wasn't finished. I wished I was tall enough to see in the window. If I walked up the steps at the door to look in, someone would probably see me. At least on the side I was somewhat concealed. I caught movement out of the corner of my eye. Carly was headed my way. She'd already seen me, though. Now I had to explain why I was standing at her trailer.

From the look on her face, I figured no matter what I said, she wouldn't be happy. She quickened her step and hurried toward the trailer. I was frozen on the spot. I didn't know if I should stay put and deal with her or run away. She'd just come to my trailer to confront me, so I decided to stay put.

"What are you doing messing around my trailer?" she asked with venom in her voice.

"I thought I saw someone looking in the window."

This came off the top of my head. Now I had to hope she believed me.

She eyed me up and down. "You are kind of nosy, aren't you?"

"I was just looking out for you. A lot of bad things have happened around here lately."

"Yes, and maybe you had something to do with them." Agitation thickened her Southern accent.

Now she was just being mean. I stepped around her. I wanted to get away from her. "Well, I could say the same about you."

She came after me. I quickened my step. This

wasn't looking good. I hoped she didn't attack me. Maybe she really was the killer. My fear kicked in. She grabbed my arm and pulled me. I almost tumbled to the ground but managed to remain upright.

"Get your hands off me," I said as I yanked away from her.

"If I catch you around my trailer again, you'll be sorry. I'll give you something to be afraid of." She placed one hand on her slender hip and pointed with her other.

She'd seemed so nice at first. Now she seemed like she wanted to kill me. This sent a shiver down my spine.

"Hey, get away from her." Caleb's voice echoed from somewhere to my left.

I glanced over and saw him walking our way.

When he approached, Carly eyed him up and down. "She was trying to break into my trailer."

"I was doing no such thing," I said.

I didn't want to mention the knife to him because he would wonder if I thought the same about him because he had a knife like that too.

Caleb touched my arm. "Come on, Celeste. Let's go."

I didn't look at Carly as we walked away. I knew she was still eyeing us. Other people were watching too. I never liked this kind of attention. I preferred to blend in with the crowd.

"Are you all right?" Caleb asked as we headed toward my trailer.

"Yes, I'm fine. She just startled me."

Now I had to explain to him exactly why I had

been at her trailer. I suppose I would have to use the same lie. I felt bad that I couldn't tell him the truth. "I thought I saw someone around her trailer too," I said. Would he believe me? He might think I was just making all of this up.

"Was it Shar?" he asked.

"I'm not sure."

Now I was blaming Shar for something she hadn't done. This was taking a wrong turn. Soon we reached my trailer.

"Have you spoken with the detective yet?" Caleb asked.

"No. I guess I should call him now," I said.

"Why don't you let me call? You have too much on your mind. I can handle this for you," he said.

"That's nice of you to offer," I said.

Was he really being nice, or did he have another motive for the call? Maybe I would call the detective anyway.

"I didn't expect to see you so soon. Were you coming back to tell me something?" I asked. He'd probably seen Elizabeth. Now he would believe me.

"I was just headed for refreshments. Would you like something?"

Where was Elizabeth? Why didn't she pop up and show herself?

"No, thanks. I just want to destress. Carly didn't hurt me, so I'll just let it go for now."

He studied my face. "If you're sure?"

I nodded. "Yes. I just want to go to bed."

"I'll check on you soon?" he asked.

"Sure. Talk to you later," I said with a wave.

Once in my trailer, I peeked out the little window. Caleb was walking down the path. I peered around to see if anyone was prowling around. All was quiet and I hoped it stayed that way. At least for the rest of the day, so that I could calm down.

After Van chowed down on his savory beef and chicken nibbles, we played for a bit until he tired and wanted to sleep on my lap. I settled down under the covers and he snuggled up beside me. There was nothing like hearing the sweet sound of his breathing in my ear. I wasn't sure of the time when I woke, but it felt as if someone was watching me. I opened my eyes. Things were still blurry, but I spotted Elizabeth by the door.

She was watching me. "Oh, did I wake you?"

"I'm not sure." She would have to answer that herself. "Did you want me to wake up?" I asked.

"Well, I have been patient," she said.

I sat up in bed. Van crawled under the covers so we wouldn't disturb him. I didn't blame him. I wanted to crawl back under there too.

"It isn't even all the way light out yet."

"Early bird gets the worm," Elizabeth said.

"I don't like worms," I said around a yawn.

I stumbled out of bed and headed for the kitchen area, which was only a few steps.

"Is something wrong, Elizabeth? Why did you wake me so early?" I spun around. "Wait a minute. I thought you would be with Caleb."

"I don't want to talk to him. I'm not happy you gave the painting of me away."

"I didn't give it away," I said as I reached for the coffee mug. "I just let him borrow it. I want him to see you so that he'll believe me. If I'm the only one who sees you, everyone will think I'm crazy."

"I'm sorry, Celeste, I don't think I feel comfortable talking with other people."

So I was the lucky one who had grabbed her attention?

She continued. "What clues have you found that will lead you to the killer? I feel as if things are getting more dangerous by the minute."

It was kind of early to think about a murder investigation. I hadn't had my coffee yet.

"Carly had a knife in her purse just like the one that was used to murder Evan. What if she has that one because she intends on killing someone else?" I asked.

"That's scary," Elizabeth said in a shaky voice.

"I noticed Caleb had a lot of cash on him. What if he has been stealing money? Evan could have found out about it and Caleb murdered him because of it," I said.

"That's a good point," Elizabeth said. "What else?"

"The new director of the fair. He said he deserved to be running things now. What if he killed Evan so he could take his job?"

"You just need to find the one clue that will lead you to the killer."

"Well, yes, that would help," I said.

My cell rang and interrupted the conversation. Elizabeth looked around for the source of the sound.

"My phone." I gestured to the counter.

She still looked as if she had no clue what I meant. I picked up the phone. Sammie was calling early. I hoped nothing was wrong.

"Are you all right?"

"I'm ready to go," Sammie said.

"Go where?"

"We are going to breakfast before you have to do the fair today. I talked with your mother and they're meeting us at your aunt's diner."

"Oh no. You know how it is when we go there with them."

"She promised she'd be on her best behavior today."

"She says that, but I'm not sure we should believe her."

"Your brothers are coming too," Sammie said.

"What? Is this a family reunion?"

"They were there and overheard the conversation. I'll be by to pick you up in fifteen minutes. Come on, you said we'd do this."

"Fine. I'll be ready."

"Was that a friend?" Elizabeth asked.

"Yes. I have to go to breakfast, so we'll have to continue this conversation later."

"Maybe I can go with you," she said.

"If you really want to go. Oh wait. I have an idea. Sammie will be here soon. She didn't believe me when I told her that I see a ghost. You should show yourself to her so she knows I'm not crazy."

"I don't know." She shivered at the thought.

"Sammie's really nice. You'll love her. After all, would I have bad taste in friends?"

She grimaced. "You seem to like everyone. Life is puppies, rainbows, and candy as far as you're concerned."

I frowned. "What makes you say that?"

"I'm observant," she said.

"What do you say? Will you pop in and say hello?" I flashed her my best sad-eyed look.

"Perhaps I will."

I supposed that was better than a no.

"Van, it's time to wake up and eat breakfast."

He didn't budge, so I peeked under the covers. He looked up at me like a teenager being woken up to go to class. My aunt had outside tables, so I would take him with me.

A few minutes later, there was a knock at the door.

"Oh, that's Sammie. Stay right there."

Elizabeth didn't respond. I hoped that was a yes. Wait until Sammie saw the ghost. I opened the door.

"Are you ready?" Sammie asked.

"Almost. Can you come in?"

She looked at me suspiciously. Sammie couldn't see into the kitchen area unless she was actually inside the trailer. She walked up the steps and came in. I watched her expression. When would she look over and spot Elizabeth?

"Are you ready?" Sammie asked again. "What more do you need to do?"

Why wasn't she looking over at Elizabeth? I glanced over toward the kitchen. Elizabeth was gone.

I looped my purse over my shoulder and grabbed Van. "I'm ready."

Sammie rubbed Van's head. "Hey, buddy. Are you ready to share my breakfast?"

Van barked. Sammie had parked her truck near my trailer. She drove a big red pickup. It was great for hauling the antiques she found for her shop. We climbed in and headed for the diner.

"It seems as if something is wrong. You're still upset about the murder," Sammie said.

"That's part of it. I wanted you to see the . . ." I realized Elizabeth was sitting between Sammie and me.

I gasped, which made Sammie swerve.

CHAPTER 15

Travel trailer tip 15:
Don't forget to be adventurous sometimes.

After she'd corrected the truck, Sammie said, "What in the world is wrong? Why did you do that?"

Sammie looked over and screamed. Again, she swerved the truck. Several cars honked at us.

"Who is that?" Sammie asked breathlessly.

"This is Elizabeth. I'm so glad you can see her."

"I'm not glad I can see her. I'm freaking out."

"Maybe you should pull over until the shock has worn off."

Sammie merged over to the side of the road and turned on the flashing lights.

"Who is this woman?" Sammie had her hand on the door handle.

"She's the ghost I told you about."

"She wasn't here when we got in the truck."

"I know."

"How did she get in here?" Sammie's hand remained on the handle.

Elizabeth focused straight ahead at the road. I

knew it had taken a lot of courage for her to do this. Now I needed to calm Sammie down.

"Does she speak?" Sammie asked.

"Well, she has in the past. Elizabeth, do you want to say hello to my best friend Sammie?"

Elizabeth looked over at Sammie.

"Hello," she said softly.

Sammie's eyes widened.

"Good morning," Sammie said.

"Do you believe me now?" I asked.

Sammie released a deep breath. "I have no choice *but* to believe you. I can see her with my own eyes."

"She wanted to come to the diner with us," I said.

Sammie watched Elizabeth for a couple more seconds before putting the truck in Drive.

"Well, we should get there." Sammie didn't sound too sure of that comment.

Nevertheless, Sammie merged back onto the road. She peeked over at Elizabeth every few seconds. Soon, we pulled into the diner's parking lot. Memories of Caleb popped into my mind. I wondered what he was doing. Was he really the killer? I hoped not. Sammie pulled the truck into a parking space and put it in Park. Once she turned off the ignition, she peered over at Elizabeth again.

"Shall we go inside? This is exciting," Elizabeth said.

"Will you be eating with us this morning?" Sammie asked hesitantly, as if she might be afraid of the answer.

Elizabeth laughed. "No, I'm just here for the company."

We hopped out of the truck but stopped short

when we spotted Elizabeth already standing on the patio.

"That was weird," Sammie whispered. "You could have warned me that was going to happen. I almost wrecked the truck."

"I didn't know she was going to do that."

Sammie touched my arm. "Listen, Celeste, I'm sorry I didn't believe you at first."

"I knew you didn't, but I understand. It's hard to believe," I said.

I placed Van on the ground and held his leash. He sniffed the nearby flowers while Sammie and I talked.

"You don't know why she's here?"

"I think it has something to do with the images I showed you that I've unknowingly been painting within my art."

"This is strange." Sammie blew the bangs out of her eyes.

"Are you all going to stop gossiping and join us for breakfast?" Grandma Judy waved at us.

She had no idea Elizabeth was standing right there.

"How can they not see her?" Sammie asked.

"I think she makes herself visible to those she wants to see her."

"Well, that's a handy trick," Sammie said.

"Let's get breakfast before we get in trouble," I said.

Sammie and I walked the rest of the way to the patio.

"What's so important that you kept us waiting?" my mother asked as she eyed us suspiciously.

"We were discussing art," I said.

My mother shook her head. "There's time for that later. Your brothers are getting anxious waiting for food."

My gaze traveled to my brothers. Stevie and Hank were holding their forks. Sammie and I sat down at the table. My mother was across from us, with my brothers on either side. My father sat at one end and my grandmother sat at the other.

"Aunt Patsy's making breakfast for us," my mother said.

Aunt Patsy insisted on having us come to the diner to eat at least once a month. At least she had help at the diner on busy days. The diner had increased business this past year, and Aunt Patsy had hired two cooks and a handful of waitresses and waiters. Elizabeth was peering in the diner's window.

"Aren't we going inside?" she asked.

Sammie and I exchanged a look. Was I supposed to answer Elizabeth? Of course I hadn't told the others about her yet. My brothers would make fun of me.

"Who do you two keep looking at?" my mother asked as she looked over her shoulder.

I had decided I wouldn't tell her now. It was best if I waited for a time when we were alone. Meaning I didn't want to tell her in front of my brothers. Memories of them making fun of me flashed back. I didn't want to give them ammunition. They still looked for ways to tease me every chance they got.

"Celeste and I have been talking with a ghost," Sammie blurted out.

My brother Stevie spit out his water. They all laughed.

"What in the world are you all talking about?" my mother asked.

"Have you been drinking already?" my father asked.

"Of course not. You know I don't drink," I said.

"Celeste's painting had mysterious images and a ghost showed up. She's here right now. She's standing behind you." Sammie's words gushed out like a busted water pipe.

My mother looked over her shoulder. "I don't see a thing. Are you all sure you're okay?"

I glared at Sammie. I could have told her this was how my family would react.

"I believe you," my grandmother said.

"Can you see her, Grandma?" I asked.

"I sense her," she said. "When she wants to show herself, she will."

"That's exactly what Elizabeth said," Sammie said.

"Who is Elizabeth?" my mother asked.

"She's the ghost."

"You know her name?" Stevie asked around a laugh.

My aunt Patsy came outside with a tray full of food. I jumped up to help her.

"Sit back down," she snapped.

She said that every single time. That still didn't stop me from trying to help. She was the most stubborn person I knew. She set down the plates and looked around the table.

"Is there anything else I can get for you all?"

"Yeah, a psychiatrist for Celeste," my brother Hank said.

Aunt Patsy swatted at his shoulder.

"The girls have been telling us about the ghost that's here with them," my mother said.

"Is that right?" Aunt Patsy raised an eyebrow. "Where did you meet this ghost?"

Sammie recited the whole story over again.

Aunt Patsy placed her hands on her hips. "I believe in ghosts. If they say they saw one, I believe them."

"I want to see these mysterious images you're talking about," my mother said.

"What mysterious images?" Aunt Patsy asked.

"The spirits are talking with her," my grandmother said.

She was busy eating her pancakes. Grandma didn't always act as if she was even listening to the conversations.

"Why do you say that, Grandma?" I asked.

"That's what they do."

I wasn't sure if she had some knowledge that led her to say that, and she wasn't sharing the full details.

"What does the ghost look like?" Aunt Patsy asked.

"She's beautiful," Sammie said.

"Oh, a babe ghost," Hank said.

I tossed a grape at him.

"She has dark hair and is always wearing a gorgeous dress from the turn of the twentieth century," Sammie said.

"Do you know where she lived or anything else about her?" my mother asked.

"We don't know anything else about me yet," Elizabeth said as she sat in the chair next to my mother.

Sammie and I looked at each other.

"What is it?" my mother asked with a raised eyebrow.

"The ghost just answered you," I said.

My mother looked around. "Where is she?"

"She's sitting right beside you." I gestured with my fork.

"You all are bonkers," Stevie said.

"Don't call your sister crazy," Aunt Patsy said.

"I should leave. I'm causing a lot of drama," Elizabeth said.

"Don't worry, there's always drama in my family."

"What did she say?" my mother asked.

"She's worried that's she's causing us to argue," I said.

"Oh no, honey, we're always like this," my mother said, looking around for the ghost.

"Maybe we should change the subject for a bit," I said.

"How's the art fair? Are you making any money?" my father asked. He was always right to the point.

"A little," I said.

He frowned but didn't say anything else about my lack of funds.

My father was distracted by asking Stevie and Hank questions about their work. Thank goodness I was off the hook for a bit. My mother was talking to Sammie about antiques. During the bit of a reprieve, I enjoyed my French toast. Elizabeth sat in the chair watching all of us. She smiled, and oddly looked as if she was having fun.

My brief time of relief came to a screeching halt when I spotted Caleb walking across the parking lot.

"Hey, isn't that the guy you came here with?" Aunt Patsy pointed.

"Yes, that's him," I said under my breath.

My whole family turned to look at him. At that time, he realized he was being watched. He hadn't noticed me at first, but soon his gaze fell on mine. A big smile spread across his face.

"Well, my, my, isn't he handsome," my grandmother said.

"I don't like the guy," Hank said.

"Oh, you don't like any of Celeste's suitors," my grandmother said with a wave of her hand.

"Suitors?" I asked with a laugh. "I wouldn't call him a suitor."

"Okay, I'll call him your boyfriend."

"Oh, he's definitely not my boyfriend. Just a friend," I said.

"Too bad," my mother said.

Caleb walked over to us.

"Good morning, Celeste," he said with another big smile.

"I didn't expect to see you here," I said.

"Would you like to join us for breakfast?" My mother gestured to the chair next to her, where Elizabeth sat.

"Oh, I had planned on just picking up something to go," Caleb said.

That was probably for the best. My brothers were already scrutinizing him. They would be nice, but they would also probably embarrass me.

My mother stood and walked over to Caleb. "Oh, we insist that you join us. See, there's an empty chair just waiting for you."

"Actually . . ." Sammie didn't finish her words.

CHAPTER 16

Travel trailer tip 16:
Don't neglect your friends and family while living
in your travel trailer. You may not have room for the
whole gang—but you can still stay in touch.

My mother guided Caleb toward Elizabeth's chair. Frowning, Elizabeth got up just before Caleb sat down. He smiled at me. I introduced everyone to him.

"It's nice to meet you all. Thanks for inviting me to join you."

He might wish he'd been uninvited soon after experiencing my family.

"Help yourself to the food." My dad gestured without looking at Caleb.

"What do you do, Caleb?" Stevie asked.

"Wood sculptures," Caleb said while taking some of the pancakes from the platter.

"That's what you do full time?" The little scar on Stevie's lip became more noticeable as he frowned. He'd bitten into an electrical cord as a baby. My mother said that was why he was so good at fixing electronics. I was pretty sure that had nothing to do with his electrical talent, but maybe I was wrong.

"I thought you meant at the craft fair. No, I'm a salesman full-time," Caleb said.

"You are?" I asked with a frown.

Now my family knew that I had very few facts about Caleb. That wouldn't sit well with them. They stared at him as if he'd just said he was an alien from a faraway planet.

"How did you meet Celeste?" my mother asked. She already knew the answer.

This would be awkward. Would he tell the truth?

"We met at the fair," Caleb said.

That was the truth, but he'd left out the bad part. My mother and father exchanged a look.

"Where at the fair? Are your booths beside each other?"

They knew we were hiding something.

"Actually, we met during the murder crime scene." Caleb looked at my mother and father.

My mother dropped her fork. "What does that mean?"

My brothers leaned forward in their chairs to hear every word Caleb had to say.

"Celeste had just discovered the body and I was walking over there and bumped into her."

"Well, there's a story to tell your grandchildren. 'Our eyes met over the corpse and we knew it was love,'" Stevie said.

I glared at him. Why was he even mentioning grandchildren? I never said I was even dating Caleb. Much less marriage and children.

"This is a morbid subject over breakfast," my mother said.

"You're right. I apologize," Caleb said.

"Actually, I find it fascinating," my grandmother said. "I want to hear about this murder investigation."

"Yeah, have you spoken with that detective lately?" Sammie asked.

"What detective?" my mother asked.

"He's been around the fair quite a bit," Caleb said.

"Does he have any idea who did it?" my grandmother asked.

"If he does, he hasn't told me," I said.

My grandmother watched me. "But you have some idea who did it, don't you?"

I avoided looking at Caleb. "It could be any of a number of people."

"Tell us about them," Hank said.

"Celeste has seen one of the vendors messing around trailers," Caleb said.

Did he really have to mention that?

"What?" my mother screeched. "You have to get away from there right away."

"I agree with your mother," my father said. "You should just quit the fair."

"That's not an option," I said. "Besides, it's almost over now. What would be the point?"

"Not being killed?" Stevie pointed out.

"I've been watching out for her," Caleb said.

"I'm fine," I said.

"I think we should check out this fair," my grandmother said.

Oh no.

"I agree," my brothers said in unison.

"Sounds like a good plan," my father said.

"Okay, we'll go now," my mother said. "Is every-one finished eating?"

This probably wouldn't end well. My father got up from the table. After they cleaned up, they headed for the car.

"We'll meet you there," I said through a forced smile.

Caleb stood beside me. "I get the impression you don't want them to go."

"I love them, but they can be a bit . . ."

"Eccentric." Sammie finished the sentence for me.

I looked over my shoulder. Elizabeth was al-ready in Sammie's truck.

"Thanks for having me join you all for break-fast," Caleb said. "I'll see you later today? I have that painting of yours and I need to give it back."

That meant he'd experienced nothing and thought he'd be better off just returning the thing.

I smiled. "Yes, I'll see you later."

I hoped it was after my family had gone. Sam-mie stopped in her tracks on her way to the truck.

"Did you think she had left already?" I asked.

"I thought maybe she would leave."

"Don't let her hear you say that. It will hurt her feelings."

Sammie nodded. "Right."

"I think she was already upset because of what my family said. Leave it to them to hurt a ghost's feelings."

Sammie laughed.

We got into the truck.

"Elizabeth, did you have a nice time?" Sammie asked.

"It was lovely," she said.

"Do we have to go back to the fair?" I asked.

Sammie laughed. "I think you do."

"Is your family mad at me?" Elizabeth asked.

"Oh no, they like you," I said.

Sammie and I discussed where we thought Elizabeth came from as we headed back to the fairgrounds. Every time we mentioned a place, Elizabeth would shake her head.

"That's not it. I'll know it when I hear it."

I was running out of ideas.

"We should check out the museum. Max's friends said there's a portrait of a woman who looks just like you, Elizabeth," I said.

"What are you waiting for? Why haven't we gone there yet?"

"We could go later. Right now, I have to get back to the fairgrounds before my family does something that will land us all in jail."

"Oh . . ." Elizabeth said through pursed lips. "I don't want to go to jail. Well, how about after you say farewell to your family?"

"Sure, but we'll have to go before they close," I said.

Soon, we arrived back at the fairgrounds. Sammie pulled her truck close to the trailer and we all got out.

"Whoa, where do you think you're going?" Max waved his arms at us as he headed our way.

"Uh-oh," I said. "Here comes trouble."

"What does he want?" Sammie asked.

"Is something wrong?" I asked Max.

"You can't park that truck here. Get it out of here."

"Sorry, I didn't think it would be a problem. She's just dropping us off," I said.

Van barked at Max. He glared at Van. I didn't like the way he looked at Van.

"It's okay, Celeste, I'm leaving." Sammie glowered at Max.

He gave me the creeps and I didn't want to get into a confrontation with him. He stood there, as if waiting for her to leave.

"I'll call you in a bit," Sammie said as she climbed into her truck and revved its engine, as if expressing her disdain.

As she pulled the truck away, Max stepped closer to me. He was inches away from my face. Van was barking like crazy. I stepped back and held Van tight in my arms.

"Make sure that doesn't happen again. If it does, I'll have to ask you to leave and perhaps recommend you not attend any other craft fairs in the area," Max said through gritted teeth.

"What seems to be the problem?" Caleb called out.

I looked over my shoulder and saw him running toward us. Max backed away.

"What's the problem?" Caleb repeated, stepping close to Max. I thought he might hit him.

"She's not following the rules," Max said as he stepped back from Caleb.

Now he knew what it felt like to have someone in his face.

"I didn't know we weren't supposed to park here," I said. "There are no signs about it."

"Well, you should have known," Max said.

"Why? It's not in the page of rules I was given."

"That's Evan's fault. Things have changed now that I'm here. They changed for the better." Max stared at us before turning to walk away.

"Are you all right?" Caleb asked.

"Yes. He just scared Van."

Caleb rubbed Van's head. "It's okay, buddy, he's gone now."

"Thanks for talking to him," I said.

"It's not a problem. If he says anything else, call me, okay?"

"I will. Right now, though, I need to find my family. I don't want them to encounter Max. It likely wouldn't end well."

"Where is she?" My mother's voice echoed from somewhere nearby.

Caleb and I walked around to the front of my trailer. My entire family was standing there. Whispering, gaping mouths, and general surprised expressions covered their faces when they saw Caleb and me together.

"Well, well, well, looks like the lovebirds are busy," Stevie said in a singsong voice.

Heat rushed to my face.

"What are you all doing now? I need to get to work, y'all," I said.

"We've just been checking things out," my mother said. "We met Shar and Carly. They seem nice."

"What did you say to them?" My eyes widened.

"Nothing," my mother said.

The tone of her voice seemed too sweet. Something told me she wasn't telling the whole truth.

"Where did you see them?" I asked.

"They were at their booths when we walked by," my grandmother said.

What were the odds they would just happen to walk by there and talk with them?

"What did they say to you?" I asked.

"Just casual talk about the items they're selling," my mother said with a smile.

I eyed her suspiciously before turning my attention to the rest of the family.

"We'll get out of your hair now," my mother said.

That was her code for "I'll call you soon and get all the details."

CHAPTER 17

Travel trailer tip 17:
Learn to deal with the fact that your travel trailer
won't have all the conveniences you want.
Simplicity can be a great cure for stress.

It was a crazy idea, but I decided to do it anyway. It wouldn't be the first time I'd done something that was a little questionable. I'd been snooping around for anything connected to Evan's murder, so what was one more time going to hurt?

Going with Caleb to dinner was definitely questionable behavior. As if that wasn't enough, now I'd decided to check out his trailer. When Caleb had stopped by mine to return the painting and announced he was headed to the store for some glue for his wood carvings, I knew I had to act right away to go back to his trailer. Maybe I should have said yes so that would have kept him away longer and given me more time to snoop around. I just felt as if I hadn't gotten a good enough look the first time. Perhaps I had missed something the time before.

I wasn't going inside his trailer, though. Well, that was unless he left the door open. That would be too risky, though, right? Yes, definitely too risky. I just wanted to walk around to see if there was anything unusual.

I hoped he wasn't around, because I wouldn't know what to do it if I saw him. However, I knew he'd gone to the store for a few supplies. He'd stopped by to ask if I needed anything. It was so sweet of him to ask, and I told myself that someone that nice surely wouldn't be a murderer. Now I was using this time to spy on him. I walked down the path toward Caleb's trailer. Anxiety danced in my stomach.

Once I reached Caleb's trailer, I checked to see whether anyone was watching. Everyone around seemed busy and as if they had no clue I was even around. His tools and items were all put away. I inched over to his petite white trailer with the palm tree painted on the side for a peek inside. This thing was even smaller than mine. The Happier Camper, as it was called, was much newer than mine, though. I knew the make and model because I'd looked at one like this before buying my Shasta. Unfortunately, I was too short to see in. Now what? I made my way around the side of the trailer. Maybe there was a window on the back.

I'd just made it around the corner when I almost tripped over a trash can. Thank goodness I managed to remain upright and not land in the thing. Hmm. A trash can. Maybe there was something in there.

Had I really stooped to a whole new low? Now I was snooping around in Caleb's trash can? My hands shook as I rummaged through the wood scraps and discarded food wrappers. Every few seconds, I peered over my shoulder to see if anyone was watching me. I wasn't sure what I hoped to find in the garbage. I was desperate for some kind of clue. I wanted something to prove Caleb was innocent more than I wanted something to prove he was guilty.

I dug deeper and spotted fabric. Giving a tug, I pulled out the material and realized it was a yellow T-shirt. I almost tossed it back into the trash when I noticed the stain across the front. I would've guessed that the large red mark was paint, but as far as I knew, Caleb didn't paint his wood carvings. So that led me to only one conclusion: it was blood.

Noise from behind me caught my attention. I spun around, still holding the bloody shirt. This wouldn't look good at all. Shar was behind me. Her mane of red hair appeared unbrushed, the circles under her eyes even darker, She looked down at my hand. How would I explain this?

"I was just going through the trash looking for some rags. I can always use rags for my paintings." I attempted a weak smile.

"That doesn't make sense, but whatever," she said.

"There's not much in this one, so I'm out of luck," I said, now forcing a nervous laugh.

"That's Caleb's trash, right?" Shar pointed.

I looked at the trash can. "I suppose. I'm not sure."

Shar looked as if she had something she wanted to say, but she scanned the area first to make sure no one was listening.

"I saw him that night, you know," she said.

I raised an eyebrow. "You saw who?"

"Caleb. He was by Evan's trailer."

"Yes, I know, he got there right after I found the body," I said.

"No, I saw him before that. I just didn't think much of it at the time."

Why was she at Evan's trailer to see Caleb in the first place? "Were you going to see Evan about the incident with the tables at your booth?" I asked.

She narrowed her eyes. Instead of answering my question, she said, "It seems as if you're sneaking around Caleb's trailer." She eyed me up and down. "Just like the night you found Evan."

Was she accusing me of something?

Actually, yes, that was exactly what she was doing. Why didn't she just come out and ask me if I was the killer?

"Well, you're doing the same thing, so I can ask the same of you," I said, looking her up and down.

She glared. "How dare you. Are you saying I'm the killer?"

"Are you saying I'm the killer?" I asked.

Shar stared at me as if we were in a showdown. I kept my eyes focused on her. I couldn't let her see I was scared. I stood tall. Well, as tall as I could at five foot two, and pushed my shoulders back.

After a couple more seconds, she turned on her heel and stomped away. I'd won the stare down, and this confrontation was over.

Now I had to get back to figuring out why Caleb had a bloody shirt in his trash can. Perhaps this was the shirt he had been wearing when Evan was murdered. He could have come back to his trailer, changed clothes quickly, and dumped the shirt into the trash can before coming back to find me. But why would he go back to the scene of the crime after leaving? Unless he had forgotten something. Maybe he'd gone back to collect the murder weapon.

I held the shirt in my hands, examining it, trying to decide exactly what I was looking at. And the more I studied it, the more I thought for sure it was blood. I knew the look of paint on fabric because I had quite a bit of it on my clothing. I would have to show this to Pierce.

The sooner I got out of there, the better off I'd be. I'd only made it a couple of steps when a growl came from somewhere behind me. I froze on the spot. Should I move, run, or stay put? Was it Caleb's dog, Gum Shoe? He had seemed friendly, but if he thought I was a burglar, maybe he wouldn't be so nice.

Slowly, I turned around, and my eyes met with the dog's big brown peepers. The big German shepherd stood there glowering at me. His teeth weren't showing, which was a plus in my favor.

"Good doggy," I said in the sweetest voice possible. "Remember me? We met. I'm a good person. I'm not a burglar and certainly not a murderer."

With his eyes fixed on me, I realized he wasn't buying my assurances. Even though his glare let me know he was suspicious, I really didn't think he would bite me, so I decided to just leave him standing there. Though if Gum Shoe was here, where was Caleb? I'd never seen Gum Shoe without his leash or without Caleb.

I needed to get him back to Caleb. What would

I do with the shirt? I didn't have time to make the decision when Gum Shoe raced toward me. I screamed, thinking he was going to clamp down on my leg. But he didn't grab me. Instead, he went for the shirt in my hand. It was in his mouth now, but I was still holding the other end.

"Let go of that," I said. "I need that."

With a tight grip on the shirt, he wasn't budging. Plus, he was much stronger than me. I wasn't sure how much longer I would be able to hold on to the shirt. He was determined to get it from my hands.

"It was in the trash. You didn't want it anyway," I said, giving it another yank.

Yeah, I was playing tug-of-war with Gum Shoe for the shirt. Who would win? I was pretty confident it wouldn't be me. Yet I kept pulling on the shirt, trying to get him to release it.

"I need this shirt," I said breathlessly. It was evidence and I couldn't just let it go. I had to get it to Pierce and find out what the red stains were.

The dog growled and shook the shirt. I summoned all my strength. One big tug, and I instantly tumbled back onto the ground, losing my grip on the shirt. Now Gum Shoe had it at his feet as he sat down with his tail wagging. He'd thought we were playing a game all along.

"Celeste, are you all right?" Caleb came running to me.

Oh no. How long had he been watching? How much of that scene had he witnessed? He would see the shirt and wonder what I was doing, trying to get it away from the dog. I'd use the excuse that we'd been playing.

"I'm fine," I said, trying to laugh it off. "We were just playing a little game of tug-of-war."

Caleb scrunched his brow. Unfortunately, I knew I was going to lose the shirt because Caleb looked right at it. I climbed to my feet and brushed off my shorts.

"I don't know how he got that," Caleb said as he hurriedly reached down and grabbed the shirt.

Once he had it, he crumpled up the fabric so I couldn't see the stain on the front. Now he was acting suspicious, as if he was trying to hide something, but why? There was only one explanation I could think of.

"I suppose I should get back to my booth." I gestured over my shoulder.

Caleb frowned. "You came by to play with Gum Shoe?"

"I just stopped by to see how you were doing. Unfortunately, I have to get back now, though. I'll see you soon." My weak smile probably didn't seem genuine.

Caleb raised an eyebrow. "Yeah, I'll see you soon."

As I turned and hurried away, I knew he was still watching me.

CHAPTER 18

Travel trailer tip 18:
Remember, your dog still needs a walk even
if it's scary out there.

Instead of going back to my trailer, I decided to
swing by Shar's booth while Sammie was watching
my booth. Lucky for me, Sammie's appointments
had ended early and she'd had time to come back
to the craft fair to help me out. I wanted to see
how Shar was acting since seeing me at Caleb's
trailer. After that, I thought I would take a stroll by
Carly's setup and do the same.

Shar didn't notice me right away when I approached her booth. Customers had her attention, so I perused the tables of jewelry. She had
bracelets, necklaces, earrings, and rings. Most
were silver, but she also had pieces made of copper
and gold. She had a unique technique of using spi-
raled wires that added whimsical flair to each
piece. It set her designs apart from those of the
other vendors.

I watched to see if Shar had noticed me yet. If she'd looked my way, I hadn't noticed. She was still talking with a woman buying a silver-and-jade-beaded necklace. Something on Shar's hand caught my attention. The sun glinted off a gold ring on her finger. I distinctly remembered seeing that ring on Evan on the night we were setting up, though I hadn't remembered seeing it on him when I found his body.

Maybe I'd been so nervous when I'd found his body that I hadn't noticed the ring. Or maybe someone had taken the ring from him right after they'd murdered him. And that someone was Shar.

As if sensing my scrutiny, Shar stuck her hand in her pocket. Did she think that would make me forget what I'd seen? I couldn't stop looking now. After a few more seconds, Shar turned around, and I was sure she was taking the ring off. It looked as if she tucked it into her jeans pocket.

Sure enough, when she turned around again, the ring wasn't on her finger. Apparently, she didn't want me looking at it more closely. Now I wanted to know why she had it.

Clearly, she didn't want me to see that ring. Which led me to conclude that she must've taken it off Evan right after she murdered him that night. Okay, that was a huge assumption, and I shouldn't accuse her for sure, but I couldn't push the thought out of my head. What if that was really what had happened?

Once the customer had gone, Shar came over to me. "Is there something I can help you with?"

Trying to act casual, I pointed at a silver-and-turquoise ring in front of me. "It's really pretty."

Ugh. Why had I pointed at the ring? Couldn't I have picked a bracelet? Now she would be reminded of the ring in her pocket and that I'd seen it.

"Yes, it is," she said. "Unless you need something else, I need to get back to work."

Well, that wasn't subtle at all.

"All right. It was nice talking to you," I said.

Just because she was snippy with me didn't mean I had to stoop to her level. I would continue to be as sweet as honey. Nevertheless, this whole ring situation had added another twist to this puzzle. I'd found a bloody shirt in Caleb's trash. And now Shar with the ring. Not to mention Caleb with all that cash. But Ruth had a considerable amount of dough too.

Then there had been the scratches on Caleb's hands. And I'd seen Carly with one of those wood-carving knives. Why was everyone at the fair in to something suspicious? Didn't they know I was trying to find a killer? Actually, I hoped that whoever did it didn't know I was trying to discover their identity. Because that would definitely put my life in danger. And that was the last thing I needed right now.

I had a lot to consider. Maybe Van and I would take a stroll for dinner somewhere so I could think things through. I was getting sick of eating peanut butter. And I knew Van would love a little taste of my meal as well. Before that, though, I had one more stop to make.

As I walked toward Carly's, I ran through the list of suspects in my mind. Ruth, Max, Shar, Carly, and, sadly, Caleb were all on the list. The only person I'd met recently who wasn't a suspect was Detective Pierce Myers.

As soon as I turned the corner to approach Carly's booth, she looked my way. We made eye contact. She didn't smile, but she didn't frown either, so I guessed it could've been worse. Especially after she'd caught me digging through Caleb's trash can.

I looked at the embossed belts with antique gold buckles, and the leather-and-rope-braided bracelets designed like snakes that she had on display, making sure not to touch anything. It looked as if she was waiting for any chance to yell at me about something, or tell me to get lost. I just needed to act casual.

"May help you with something?" she asked in an extremely snippy tone.

I hoped she wasn't that way with all her customers or she would never sell a thing. Nobody wanted to buy things from a meanie. However, I wasn't going to take the time to point out the fact that she was being rude.

"I just thought I would stop by to take a look at your lovely items while I was out walking around. I've been thinking about buying a belt."

She raised an eyebrow, and I knew she was suspicious of me. Now I would have to buy a belt or she would know I was up to something.

"That one's really pretty." I pointed without

touching the brown, aged-leather belt embossed with sugar skulls.

"Yes, it's one of my favorites," she said in her same snippy tone. She'd been unpleasant since I'd met her, but she had really ramped it up now.

Thank goodness other customers came up and gave me a chance to look around a bit more without Carly scrutinizing my every move. When she wasn't looking, I inched closer to her trailer. I wasn't sure what I thought I was going to do. Perhaps look inside through the window? I wouldn't be able to see anything that way, but it made me feel as if I was trying, at least. Maybe I should go through her trash can too. I could only imagine her expression if she caught me doing that. She would freak out. Perhaps I needed to leave well enough alone and just go back to my trailer.

The customers were buying something from Carly. I knew she would be finished soon, and I wouldn't have that distraction to help me. Therefore, I had to move quickly. She had a small table next to her trailer with a lawn chair beside it. I supposed this was where she sat and worked on her items, and her general office area. She had a folder on top of the table.

As I walked by, a gust of wind blew a piece of paper from the top, and it floated onto the ground. I placed my foot on top of it so it wouldn't blow away. I thought I was doing her a favor. She probably wouldn't see it that way.

When I reached down to pick up the paper, I realized it was a map of the fairgrounds. That wouldn't have been so unusual, except Carly had marked

Evan's trailer and the area behind it, as if she was marking out a way to get to and from it. That was highly suspicious.

I placed the paper back on the table just as the customers walked away. Before Carly had a chance to say a word, I hurried away from her. I didn't dare turn around and look back to see if she was watching me. I assumed she was. I needed to get back to my trailer.

I wondered if Carly was walking behind me. I couldn't stand it any longer, so I peeked over my shoulder. Whew. Thank goodness she wasn't there.

I hurried the rest of the way to my trailer. I was almost there when I spotted Ruth and Max talking. As if they sensed me watching them, they looked over toward me and ended their conversation. Max went one way and Ruth rushed into her trailer. What was that all about?

CHAPTER 19

Travel trailer tip 19:
Try to avoid walking too close to other
people's travel trailers.

Later that night, I was just drifting off to sleep when I heard a strange noise, something like a loud thump, thump, thump. Driven by curiosity, I got out of bed and opened the door and peeked outside. It seemed as if someone was always poking around. Maybe it was the thief, waiting for another chance to steal money—or the killer, looking for another victim. The thought sent a shiver down my spine. I thought I heard Ruth call out my name, though she was nowhere in sight.

"Ruth, is that you? Are you all right?" I said into the darkness.

No answer came. The fairgrounds were dead quiet. What if she was in danger? I had to check on her. After locking the door behind me, I hurried over to Ruth's trailer. Just being outside at night gave me the creeps. There was no sign of Ruth.

However, a light was on in her trailer. It was probably just my imagination, I told myself. There was nothing to worry about. Nevertheless, I decided to check on her.

Despite the warm night, a breeze brought goose bumps to my skin. An owl hooted in the distance, breaking the eerie silence. I stepped up to Ruth's trailer and knocked on the door. As soon as my knuckles touch it, it opened.

"Hello?" I called out. "Ruth, are you there?"

I didn't want to step inside, but I needed to check on her. With a shaky hand, I eased the door open a little bit more.

"Ruth, are you here? Is everything all right?"

Still, I got no answer. This was making me nervous. I had to go inside. What if she had just forgotten to lock the door? What if she came back and caught me in her trailer? She would think I was the thief. I supposed I had no choice but to take that chance. I had to help her if she needed me. I took a couple more steps up the stairs and into her trailer.

Even with the little lamp on in the corner, the space was dark. Her living area was quite messy. Clothes were lying about on the table and chairs. Newspapers and other papers were tossed about. A blanket covered the little pullout sofa. Underneath it was a mound in the shape of a person. The cover was completely over the figure.

My heart sped up as I moved closer. Was Ruth under there? Had something happened to her? Standing over the sofa, I reached down and grabbed the cover. Ever so gently, I eased it back. Thank goodness it wasn't a body. Just more laundry. Ruth seriously needed to visit the laundromat. There were no other places for her to hide in the trailer, so it was time for me to get out of there.

Obviously, she had just left the door unlocked and forgotten to close it all the way. But she would have to do better than that, because someone was stealing money. This would be an easy target for them. I didn't want to tell her that I'd been in her trailer, but I would have to confess that I came by to check on her. I'd let her know the door had been open.

As I walked over to the door, I happened to glance down at some of the papers. A name on one of them caught my attention. It didn't read Ruth Gordon, but instead Ruth Stone. That was odd. I knew for sure she'd told me her last name was Gordon. And Gordon didn't sound anything like Stone. Maybe Ruth was divorced.

It was really none of my business. However, something about it made me suspicious. Perhaps it was because I was feeling that way about everyone at the craft fair. So many strange things had happened, I was suspicious of everyone. Nonetheless, I left the trailer and closed the door exactly as it had been when I arrived. I should have closed it all the way, but I didn't want to do that in case Ruth had left it that way on purpose. Maybe she didn't have a key. I didn't want to lock her out.

I moved down the small stairs and turned to position the door as I'd found it. Just as I turned to walk away, I spotted Ruth. The frown on her face was evident from all the way across the path. Only the moonlight lit her face. Her glare was focused on me. I hoped she didn't call the police. She would probably tell them that I'd been the one stealing all the money.

She rushed over to me as I tried to get back to my trailer.

"What do you think you were doing in my trailer? Are you the one taking the money?" she snapped.

I whipped around. "No, I am not taking money and I don't appreciate you accusing me of it." It really made me mad, because I hadn't done anything wrong. "You left your door open," I went on, "so I went to close it."

"Did you go inside?" she asked.

I just couldn't admit I'd gone in there.

"I did not go into your trailer. I wouldn't do that. I just wanted to make sure you were okay, so I cracked the door open just a little bit farther. I called out to you. Obviously, you weren't there."

"I would appreciate it if you stayed away from my trailer." She narrowed her eyes.

"No problem," I said.

"What did you want anyway?" The bite in her voice snapped right through me.

"I came by to ask if you heard that strange thumping sound. I thought you called out my name. Plus, it sounded as if someone was walking around the trailers. But maybe it was just an animal."

I'd told myself that, but I really thought it was more like the killer.

"I didn't hear anything. And I didn't call your name," she said. "If that's all you want, I'm going back inside."

Ruth turned and stomped back over to her trailer. Right before she walked inside, she looked back at me and gave me another nasty look. Clearly, she didn't want to be my friend.

CHAPTER 20

Travel trailer tip 20:
To sleep better, choose a quiet space to park your
trailer. Being next to the snack bar may be great
during the day, but not so much at night.

After the confrontation with Ruth, I couldn't sleep. Thoughts of the map, the ring, and the bloody shirt swirled in my head. My tossing and turning had disturbed Van and now he was awake too. Van jumped from his bed and over to the door. He scratched at it, indicating that he wanted to go out.

"It's late, Van," I said.

He scratched again, so I slipped on my sneakers and grabbed the leash. "All right, but we have to hurry."

Being outside at night sent a shiver up my spine. Nevertheless, nature called for Van. I opened the door and reached down to pick him up and put the leash on him. He darted out the door and down the steps.

"Van! Stop," I yelled.

He had never run out the door like that. I raced down the steps after him.

"Where are you going?"

He darted from the open area, around the old oak tree, and to the path.

"It's too dark back there, Van!"

Not to mention scary. I ran as fast as I could, but Van was faster. We were both on the path now.

"Where do you think you're going, Van? Stop!"

I knew he heard me because his ears were perked up. Evan's trailer came into view, and Van stopped. I reached down and picked him up. "You are a naughty dog," I said, attaching the leash to his collar.

As I turned to leave, I stopped in my tracks. I hadn't expected to see someone else there by Evan's trailer. Detective Pierce Myers was there too, shining a flashlight along the ground, as if searching for something.

The last thing I needed was for him to see me out and about around the trailer at night. He would think I'd come here on purpose. I wanted to avoid further questioning. But I also was curious about what he was doing. I assumed he was looking for more clues, but maybe he'd already found something. I would really love to know what that was.

Hoping to conceal my presence, I rushed behind a tree. I peeked out from around the trunk, hoping he didn't sense me watching him. I would only watch for a couple of minutes and then head back to my trailer. Part of me wanted to talk to Pierce, but I knew it was best that I didn't.

Pierce stood in front of the trailer, staring at something or nothing in particular. I had no idea. Was he putting the crime together in his mind, re-creating the scene in his head?

A low sound echoed from somewhere behind me, and I screamed out. That owl high in the tree-top had tattled on me. Pierce spun around, with his hand on his gun holster. I had to get out of there before he caught me. With Van in my arms, I turned around and took off running, but unfortunately, I couldn't get back on the path. He'd see me there, so I had to go in the grassy area.

My foot slipped on a big branch. My ankle twisted and I tumbled to the ground with a thump. I tried not to scream out this time. For someone who wanted to be quiet, I had done a poor job of it. I probably couldn't be any louder if I'd tried. I should have used a bullhorn and yelled at him. Perhaps a neon sign blinking over my head. Thank goodness Van was secure in my arms during my tumble. I tried to scramble to my feet. Before I could, footsteps sounded from right behind me.

When I looked up, my gaze locked onto Pierce's gorgeous hazel eyes.

He stretched out his hand toward me. "What are you doing out here?"

That was an interesting question. I had to decide what I was going to tell him. The truth?

"Van got away from me," I said as I got to my feet.

He lifted an eyebrow. "He just happened to come to the scene of the crime?"

"Okay, I admit it's a huge coincidence, but it's the truth. What are you doing over here?"

He didn't seem shocked that I'd asked him this question. "I wanted to take a look around. I've been thinking about what happened and wondering if I missed anything."

What was he thinking he'd missed? What did he think about finding me out here? It couldn't be good.

"Well, I should go back to my trailer now." Before he could answer, I spun around to walk away.

However, he quickly ran up beside me. "Wait just a minute, Celeste. I want to talk to you."

Ugh. That was what I was afraid of.

"Maybe there's somewhere we can go to talk?" he asked. "There's an ice cream shop around the corner that stays open until midnight."

Late-night ice cream? That was the place I'd gone with Caleb. I didn't want to go for ice cream tonight with Pierce.

"I have lemonade back at my trailer. We can sit there and talk," I said.

"That sounds nice."

This was certainly a strange outcome.

Pierce and I walked down the path toward my trailer. Van trotted on his leash between us.

"Sorry about back there at the trailer," I said. "That I screamed and scared you."

"I understand," he said. "It's just that, you know, without knowing who the killer is . . ."

"It's dangerous, right?" I asked.

"It could be," he said.

"Well, I opened the door before putting the leash on Van and he took off. That was a dumb mistake. If you knew my family, you'd understand why I don't always make the wisest decisions."

Pierce chuckled.

"It's definitely a character flaw I'm trying to remedy," I said.

"I'm not sure I'd call it a character flaw," he said. "Maybe just being stubborn."

"I'm pretty sure most people would consider that a character flaw."

"I just don't want you to be hurt," Pierce said.

When we reached the trailer, I gestured toward one of the folding chairs. "Have a seat. I'll just run in, put Van to bed, and get the lemonade."

He smiled and took a seat while I hurried inside. I still couldn't believe he was here and we were about to drink lemonade together. This was quite scary, actually. I had a feeling he would question me more about the murder. I would have to come clean about everything I knew. He wouldn't be happy I'd been withholding information. And also that I'd been snooping around more than he realized. He probably still thought that was why I was at the trailer tonight. I wouldn't be able to hide it any longer. I grabbed a couple of glasses and headed back outside.

When I handed him a glass, he said, "Thank you. It looks delicious."

I smiled as I sat down. "You're welcome."

Silence settled between us as we drank. I wasn't sure who would speak first, but I wanted to get everything out in the open. I'd spill everything I knew. After all, that had to be why he was here.

"You know I was snooping around tonight," I said. I felt better already, getting this off my chest and telling the truth. Well, some of the truth.

Pierce studied his glass for a few seconds and then said, "Yes, I'm aware."

"There are some other things I should tell you." He looked at me strangely.

"Well, first of all, I found a map at Carly's trailer." I rushed the words before I chickened out.

"And how did you find that?" he asked with suspicion in his voice.

"Let's just say it happened to jump out at me."

"Okay, and what about the map?"

"Well, the map was of Evan's trailer. It marked the path to get to and from it. I just thought that was suspicious."

"That is," he said. "What else?"

"Shar had a ring on her finger. I know for sure it was Evan's. I saw him wearing it and he told me he'd designed it."

"How long have you known about this?" he asked.

"Oh, I just found out not long ago. I would've told you. I was going to, but I just didn't have a chance."

He didn't look as if he believed me. "All right. Is that it?" he asked. "It sounds like you have quite a list."

I released a deep breath. "Also, it's Caleb." I hated to tell him this part, but I knew I couldn't leave it out either.

"Okay, and what about Caleb?"

"I found a shirt, and I'm almost sure it had blood on it." I couldn't believe I'd actually told him. "Now, maybe it was just his blood, but maybe you could look into that and make sure. It could be evidence."

"Wow, you have been busy," he said.

"They just kind of fell into my lap."

"I'm sure," he said. "Have you always wanted to be a detective?"

Now I was blushing. I hoped he couldn't see it in the dim light. "Well, no, not always," I said. "I'm just naturally inquisitive, that's all."

"Right," he said with a smile.

"What about you? Have you always wanted to be a detective?"

He took another drink of the lemonade. "This stuff is really good."

"Thanks. It's my aunt Patsy's recipe. She owns the Paradise Café."

"Oh, yeah, I've been to that place. Great burgers."

As he said that, Caleb came to mind, and I recalled how much he'd loved the cheeseburgers.

"But back to the detective thing, I suppose I knew when I was about seven or eight years old that I wanted to help people solve crimes. I saw a detective show on television, and after that, I always had an interest."

"We have something in common. I knew what I wanted to do at an early age too," I said.

"You did? How long have you been painting?" Pierce asked.

I explained to him about painting from a young age, but I didn't want to bore him too much. I contemplated telling him about my hidden talent of adding images within paintings, but I figured maybe that would be too much. So I kept that part quiet.

Movement caught my attention, and Pierce noticed it right away too. Caleb was walking down the path. Gum Shoe was with him. I guessed they were out for a late-night potty break. Caleb saw Pierce and me sitting at the trailer having a glass of lemonade. I knew by the look on his face that he was surprised and also maybe a bit jealous of Pierce. After all, we had gone out on a couple of dates to the café and the ice cream shop.

When Caleb realized I saw him, he turned around, heading back the other way. That kind of made me sad, but Pierce and I had only been discussing the case. Okay, we had been talking about more than that, but I digress.

Caleb had barely disappeared from view when Pierce pushed to his feet. "I should go. It was nice talking to you, Celeste. Please be careful."

I took the glass from his outstretched hand. "I promise I'll be careful. Are you going to check out the leads I gave you?"

"I'm on it. Again, be careful." He touched my chin with his index finger.

My stomach fluttered with his touch. I watched as Pierce walked down the path. Was he going to speak with Caleb now?

CHAPTER 21

Travel trailer tip 21:
Make sure to secure everything inside the trailer
in case you need to make a quick getaway.

The next morning, I received a call from Sammie.

"I need you to meet me out by the street," Sammie said when I answered.

"What's going on, Sammie?" I asked. "Where are you?"

"I'm waiting out here by the entrance to the fairgrounds. I want you to go somewhere with me."

"Why don't you drive up here?" I asked.

"No way do I want to encounter that man again," she said.

I totally understood why she wouldn't want to see Max. "Okay, but where are we going?" I asked.

"It's a surprise," she said.

Sammie knew I didn't like surprises. Nevertheless, she knew I'd do it. "Okay, I'll be right there."

I picked up Van and headed out of the trailer. While I walked toward the street, I kept my eye out for Max. I didn't want another confrontation with

him. Also, I didn't want to see Carly or Shar snooping around. All of them creeped me out. Not to
mention every time I stepped out of my trailer,
Ruth seemed to be watching me. Soon, I reached
the street and spotted Sammie's truck. I climbed
in with Van.

Sammie looked around. "Where is Elizabeth?"

"I don't know. She doesn't always pop up." I
buckled my seat belt.

"Did you ask her to come?"

"Well, no. You didn't tell me to," I said. "You're
acting strange. What's going on with you?"

She cranked the truck and pulled away from the
curb. "I hoped she would come with us."

I never tired of seeing the lush, green, tree-
covered, cloud-topped mountains as the backdrop
of my life. We drove down the main drag in town,
but the peaks and the forest painted scenery be-
yond all the shops and entertainment.

"Again, where are we going?" I asked.

"Okay, just hear me out. I thought we could see
a psychic medium." Sammie waved at a car as she
drove by. "That was Morgan Whiteman. Remember, I used to work with her at Rite Aid?"

I knew Sammie's tactic. She'd try to make this
less of a big deal but adding casual talk after saying
something outrageous.

"Why would I see a psychic? And yes, I remember her. She ate the cheese sandwich you left in
the break room."

"I think the psychic could tell us about Elizabeth." Sammie stopped at a red light.

The Gatlinburg Space Needle was on the right,
an observation tower that overlooked downtown

and the Smoky Mountains. Glass elevators carried people all the way to the top.

"We can just ask Elizabeth what we want to know." I tapped my fingers against the leather seat.

Van barked, as if agreeing with me.

"We could ask her why we're seeing Elizabeth." Sammie pressed the gas when the light turned green.

We cruised by the Ripley's Believe it or Not! Museum. The large, red-brick building appeared as if it might be falling apart, but it was designed that way on purpose. My brothers had taken me there years ago. They'd wanted to see the shrunken heads and cannibal skulls.

"Do you think she can tell us why?" I asked.

"It's worth a try, don't you think?" Sammie asked.

"Yes, I suppose that's true."

"Good. I think this will be enlightening."

"I've never been to a psychic before," I said.

"Me neither." Sammie made a left turn.

A short distance later, we pulled up in front of a white cottage. A large sign in the front yard announced the name Madame Gerard next to a caricature of a woman holding a crystal ball.

"Well, this should be interesting," I said.

Sammie pulled in and shut off the truck. The neon-red "Open" sign glowed from the front window. We got out of the truck and walked up to the front door. A sign above the doorbell instructed us to ring for service. I was a bit anxious because I wasn't sure what to expect.

"The things you get me in to," I whispered.

"Me? You're the one who brought a ghost to my truck."

"Touché," I said.

The door rattled, as if someone was unlocking it. The action was taking quite a bit of time.

"She must have a lot of locks," I whispered. "Why does she need so many?"

The door opened to reveal a woman who had long blond hair and wore a long, red-and-black dress.

"May I help you?" She eyed us up and down.

"Yes, we're here to see Madame Gerard." Sammie's voice wavered, as if she wasn't all that confident about this trip after all.

"Are you here for a reading?" the woman asked.

Sammie shifted a glance my way. "Yes, that's what we're here for."

"I've never done anything like this before," I said.

Madame Gerard soaked in my appearance. "All right. Come on in."

With a wave of her hand, she stepped out of the way and opened the door wider. Sammie and I entered, although I let her go first. There was a small hallway with rooms to the left and to the right. She gestured for us to go to the room on the right. It was a typical living room, with a sofa and chairs, but there was also a round table in the middle. Wooden chairs surrounded it. There was a crystal ball in the middle.

"Please have a seat at the table," she instructed us.

Even though I'd seen a ghost now, and Sammie had seen the ghost as well, I didn't necessarily believe in psychics. But I would give it a shot and see what she had to say. Sammie and I sat next to each other at the table. The psychic sat across from us.

"Would you like the tarot cards or a palm reading? Or maybe my crystal ball?" she asked.

"Well, actually, we're here because . . . well . . ." I stumbled over my words.

Sammie and I exchanged a look. I was going to say she should do all the talking.

"We've seen a ghost. And we just want to know more information about her, or maybe why we're seeing the ghost," Sammie said.

The lady stared at us. "I see." Her attention moved to me. I shifted in my chair. I was kind of thinking about leaving.

"It's her," she said as she pointed at me.

"Excuse me?" Now I really wanted to get out of there. The scowl on her face told me she might be angry with me.

"Did I do something wrong?" I asked.

"You did nothing wrong," she said. "You have a special talent."

"Can you elaborate on that?" I asked.

"You paint the spirits and they come alive."

With her question came a jolt of adrenaline. How did she know this?

"It's true, isn't it?" she asked with a tilted smile. She was proud of her astute assessment.

"I don't know why the spirit is there," I said with a weak voice.

"But you've recently painted images within your paintings?" she asked.

"Yes, but how do you know that?" I turned my attention to Sammie. "Did you tell her?"

Sammie held up her hands. "I don't know her. This is the first time I've ever seen her. I promise."

"This is freaking me out. I refuse to believe you know this. Someone had to have told you," I said.

Madame Gerard pushed to her feet. "Thank you for coming. You can pay me now."

"Wait," Sammie said in a panic. "You haven't told us how you know that yet. We don't know why the ghost appeared."

Madame Gerard glared at me. "I don't like being accused of shady practices. I am a psychic medium. The spirits talk to me."

"That's how you know about what Celeste does? The spirits told you about it? Who is the spirit?" Sammie's voice was full of excitement.

This was interesting news, of course, but I was still so shocked, I couldn't think of what to say.

"Well, the spirit is gone now. You broke the line of communication with your negativity." Madame Gerard sat back down at the table. She looked right at me, letting me know it was me who was responsible for this.

"Can you get the spirit to come back?" Sammie asked.

Madame Gerard pushed up the sleeves of her billowy blouse and adjusted her bangle bracelets. "I can try. You must force out all the negative thoughts in your head."

I released a deep breath and tried to clear my mind. I really did want to know what else she had to say. Was there another spirit around? I assumed she was talking about Elizabeth, but if it was her, why wouldn't she just appear here and talk to me?

"It will be easier if we hold hands and close our

eyes." Madame Gerard gestured for us to hold her hands.

"Is this like a séance?" Sammie asked.

"I prefer to call it communicating with the dearly departed," Madame Gerard said.

So it was a séance. Sammie took my left hand and I grasped Madame Gerard's hand with my right. A ring was on every one of her fingers.

"I call to the spirit who was just here. We need your help. Can you answer the questions for us?"

I lifted one eyelid for a peek. Madame Gerard's eyes were closed. Sammie had lifted one eyelid and looked at me too. I wished the spirit would just appear, like Elizabeth. It would be much easier to speak with her like that than wait for Madame Gerard to relay the message.

Madame Gerard was silent. Had she fallen asleep? It looked as if the spirit wasn't coming back for a chat. If the spirit was that sensitive, did I really want a message? Should I interrupt and ask her what was going on now? She would only get mad. Van was sitting on the chair next to me. His eyes were closed too. Was he just doing that because he saw us, or was he trying to help with the séance?

"The spirit says you have psychic abilities and that is why you are painting the images. You don't even realize you're doing it. The spirits are helping you do it. When they want to appear, they will have you paint their image," Madame Gerard said.

"Just like with Elizabeth," I whispered. "Who is the ghost speaking with you?"

"She won't tell me her name. She says she will appear soon." Madame Gerard's eyes remained shut.

"What does she look like?" Sammie asked.

"She has blond hair and a thin face with blue eyes."

"That doesn't sound like Elizabeth," Sammie said.

Did this mean another ghost would appear soon?

"She's gone now," Madame Gerard said, releasing our hands.

She pushed to her feet and walked over to the candles on the nearby table. I supposed that meant our reading was over. It was probably for the best.

I picked up Van. "Thank you for the information."

Madame Gerard remained quiet.

Sammie and I walked to the door. Van was in my arms. When I reached the door, I peeked over my shoulder. Madame Gerard was right behind me.

She touched my arm. "Come back and see me sometime, all right?"

I was surprised. I thought for sure she didn't like me.

"Okay, I'll do that." Uncertainty filled my words.

A hint of a smile crossed her lips, but it faded quickly, making me wonder if I'd really seen it at all. The prolonged eye contact with her arctic-blue eyes sent a chill down my spine. Was there something more? What she wanted clicked in my mind.

"Oh, I forgot to pay you," I said, reaching into my purse.

She took the cash but remained silent.

Sammie and I stepped out onto the porch. Madame Gerard closed the door behind us. The clicking of many locks sounded from the other side. Why did she have so many locks? Sammie and I exchanged another look, but we didn't say anything. Maybe it was better if we didn't know the reason.

We got back into the truck and pulled away. When I glanced back, I spotted Madame Gerard peeking out the window. Was she making sure we'd left?

"What do you think about what she said?" Sammie asked as we headed back toward the fairgrounds.

"I don't know what to think," I said. "What she says matches with the crazy things that have been happening. I wish I knew why, though."

"Maybe she will be able to explain that later. She asked you to come back sometime. Do you think you'll see her again?" Sammie asked.

"I suppose I am curious," I said.

"You should definitely go back soon," Sammie said.

I supposed that was what best friends were for. To talk us into things we didn't want to do, knowing it might actually be good for us. Sammie had persuaded me to visit the psychic and now I was thinking that might have been a good thing. She had revealed that I had a special talent: I painted the spirits and they spoke to me.

How would Madame Gerard have known that if she wasn't a true psychic?

CHAPTER 22

Travel trailer tip 22:
Sometimes you need all hands on deck.

When we arrived back at the fairgrounds, it was in a bit of chaos. Police cars crowded the parking lot. Soon the craft fair would be over, and honestly, I was surprised the police hadn't shut it down already because the event was basically over.

"This is beginning to be a regular occurrence around here. I doubt people will want to come around with this much crime," Sammie said as she parked the truck. She'd made sure to park in the designated area this time.

"What do you think is going on?" I asked as I picked up Van. "I hope it's not another murder."

Sammie's eyes widened. "Do you really think it could be?"

"Anything is possible," I said.

As we neared the area where people were gathered, I asked a couple of vendors if they knew what had happened.

"Someone stole money again," the tall, middle-aged blonde said.

"Who was the victim this time?" I asked.

"I believe it was Wanda, the woman who makes Native American beaded jewelry."

I'd seen her work, and we'd had a great conversation about her jewelry and how she used copper and carved beads. These items had been used as far back as prehistoric times.

"That's terrible," I said.

"I hope they find the rotten scoundrel who's responsible for this." A woman with a tangle of auburn hair spilling past her shoulders rubbed her arms as if she was fighting off a chill. The hot temperature let me know her goose bumps came from fear.

"I heard the police are closing in on a suspect for this, and the murder," the blonde said with a click of her tongue.

"But they didn't catch the person this time?" I asked.

"Not that I'm aware of," the woman said. "Though I think they should tell us more about what's going on. It would ease our minds to know if the murderer has been caught, or at the very least is close to being behind bars."

"But you heard they were close to finding the culprit?" I asked the other woman.

"Well, that could just be hearsay. You know how people like to gossip."

Yes, I certainly knew that all too well.

"I wonder if I can go to my trailer," I said.

"Probably not until they finish checking out the crime scene," Sammie said.

Wanda's booth was close to mine, and that was scary. To think, while we'd discussed her making the beaded jewelry in the same tradition as her Cherokee ancestors, the perpetrator could have been spying on us. After all, I'd sensed being watched during the entire conversation.

As we stood chatting, I spotted Caleb in the distance, standing off by himself by a tree. A flash of the time I'd seen he had all that cash in his pocket came to mind. I tried to push it away. Caleb really was too nice to do anything dishonest.

Looking farther, I spotted Max walking to the left of the group. The detective walked up behind him, stopped him, and they talked. I supposed he was speaking with him about the crime. Caleb watched the detective too.

"Celeste, I need to leave," Sammie said. "Do you want to come with me tonight? There's no sense in you staying here."

"I'd rather stay here with my trailer and my paintings," I said. I loved the trailer and worried about leaving it for too long. It was part of me now. "I'm sure things will be fine. The police are here."

"Yes, but they have to leave sometime."

"Van and I will be in the trailer, so we'll be fine."

"If you're sure, but call me when you find out anything or if you need anything at all," Sammie said.

"I promise I will." After hugging Sammie goodbye, I turned my attention back to the scene.

The area near my trailer was still blocked off. Curious about what Max was up to, I walked around the edge of the taped-off area. I thought the police should pay more attention to him. After all, everyone was a suspect as far as I was concerned.

Max walked all the way over to his trailer and went inside. Now what? I wanted to know what he was up to. I supposed peeking inside would be bad. If the police caught me doing that, it wouldn't look good. They'd probably handcuff me and take me to jail. Yet I had to take a look. Something about him made me uncomfortable.

I eased over to the trailer, looking over my shoulder to make sure that no one was watching me. The trailer's front windows were open. How could he relax when all this chaos was going on around him? When I was next to the trailer, I stood on my tiptoes so I could see into the window.

Max sat at a tiny table. If he looked over and saw me, I would be in big trouble. I didn't want to be banned from the grounds for future craft fairs, but it would be worth it if it meant I got to the bottom of this crime. Max was counting money, placing each crisp bill onto the table in front of him. Where had he gotten so much cash? I was pretty sure the detective should know about this.

"What are you doing?" a male voice asked.

I turned around so quickly, I fell to the ground. Luckily, I caught myself with the palms of my hands. Caleb rushed over and helped me to my feet. I wiped off my hands on my pants.

"What are you doing?" he asked again.

My face was probably red with embarrassment. I motioned for him to follow me away from the trailer.

We'd only made it a couple of steps when I said, "Stop. Let's go back. I want you to see something."

He hesitated, but followed me back to the trailer. I pointed, and he looked through the window for a minute.

"That's a lot of cash," he said.

"Yes, it is kind of odd that he has that much money."

I wondered if Caleb was thinking the same thing about himself. After all, I'd caught him with a bunch of money as well. I never carried more than fifty bucks around with me. I always took the money I earned for the paintings I sold and deposited it into the bank as soon as possible. I hoped the other vendors were doing that as well now.

"Who's out there?" Max asked in a loud, booming voice.

Caleb grabbed my hand, and we ran around the side of the trailer. I heard the trailer door open and knew he was looking for someone. We stopped running, trying to catch our breath.

"Hold it right there," a new male voice said.

I looked over my shoulder. This didn't look good.

"Why are you running away?" Detective Pierce Meyer asked with a puzzled look on his face.

I wasn't sure he'd believe anything I had to say.

"We were trying to get away from Max's trailer," I said.

"And why were you doing that?" he asked.

"Well, that's a good story," I said.

"I'm sure it is. Would you care to share it with me?"

Caleb didn't look too thrilled about talking to the detective. But he had caught us acting strangely, so it wasn't as if we had a choice.

"Well, I saw into his trailer and he had a bunch of cash. I think he's the one taking the money."

Why was I telling on Max, but not telling on Caleb? That didn't seem quite fair. I had to tell the detective about Caleb too, right?

"And why did you happen to be looking into his trailer? Is this something you do often?"

"Well, no, absolutely not, other than that one time," I said.

Pierce stared at me.

"I was just suspicious of him, so I felt like I needed to look."

"You need to let us handle the investigation. It could be dangerous for you," he said.

"I realize that, but it's over with now, so I think you really should ask him about the money."

"All right, we can look into that," he said.

I was hoping he meant right now. Because maybe Max was planning on taking off with all that cash.

"Perhaps you all should go back on the other side of the crime tape."

"Yeah, we can do that, can't we, Caleb?" I said.

Caleb and I walked over and got back on the other side of the tape. Pierce went up to Max's trailer and knocked on the door.

"What if Max has a gun?" I whispered.

"I think we should probably duck if that happens," Caleb said.

"Well, yeah, of course, but I don't want the detective to get shot trying to look into this," I said.

"Things will be fine. Don't worry." Caleb touched my arm for reassurance.

We waited with bated breath for that door to open. Luckily, Max didn't have a gun or any other weapon. As the detective talked to him, I wished we could hear what they were saying. The detective must be asking about the money. Max looked in our direction.

After a few seconds, he focused his attention back on the detective. The detective must have told him that we had told him about the money. Max would be angry now. After a few seconds, the detective turned around and headed back toward us. Max closed the door.

"Why did you tell him that we told you?" I asked.

He held up his hands. "Calm down. I didn't mention you."

"Why did he look at us?" I asked.

"I'm not sure. I didn't use your name at all. I told him that I saw him with money."

"You did that?" I asked. "That was so nice. Thank you."

Caleb glanced at me with a funny look.

"What was his excuse for having so much cash?" I asked.

"He said it's his money and he hadn't had a chance to go to the bank. We really have no reason to suspect him," the detective said.

"Listen, I really should get going," Caleb said. "Thanks for checking into that for me, Detective. I'll see you later, Celeste, okay?"

"Sure, I'll see you later." I waved. It was strange he'd left so abruptly.

When Caleb was out of earshot, the detective said, "What was that all about?"

"I didn't want to say anything, but I suppose I have to now. The other day, Caleb wanted to buy one of my paintings. He had a wad of cash. It was right after one of the episodes."

"I wish you had told me that sooner," he said.

"I just didn't think Caleb was capable of anything like that. Though after telling you about Max, I figured I should mention it. Needless to say, it's been bothering me. If you talk to him, don't say the same thing you told Max. There's no way he'd believe you."

"I'll think about what to do and take care of it, okay? I won't tell him that you said anything."

"I appreciate that, thank you."

At least the crowd had dispersed now, and the police were headed away too.

"Can I walk you back to your trailer?" he asked.

"That would be great. I think Van is getting a little tired."

"He's had quite an eventful day, I'm sure."

He only knew half of it. He didn't know we'd been to a psychic before this. And he knew nothing about the ghost.

The detective and I walked up the path toward my trailer. I wasn't sure I was happy that the police had left as I thought about being all alone in the trailer for the night. Would the criminal strike again?

"Do you think the thief is the same person who murdered Evan?" I asked.

"It's hard to say for sure. But it's definitely something we're looking at," he said.

"I wish I had a clue that linked them."

"You're really in to solving this, aren't you?" he asked.

"Well, I found Evan and, in a way, I feel like it's my responsibility to solve the case."

"You know that's not true," Pierce said.

"Maybe so, but it would make me feel better."

Would Elizabeth be standing by the trailer waiting for me? Apparently, the answer to that was yes. I spotted her right away when we walked up.

She popped up beside Pierce. "Tell him about me."

I tried not to look at her, but she waved her arms.

"I know how you feel, Celeste. Every case I don't solve feels as if I've let the victim and the victim's family down. It comes with the job."

Elizabeth reached out and ran her hand along his stubbled, sculpted jaw. Pierce scrunched his brow and looked in her direction.

"Is everything okay?" I asked.

An icy-cold touch moved across my cheek.

"Maybe if you all would pay attention to me, I wouldn't have to do that," Elizabeth said.

I glared at her.

Pierce noticed my reaction and glanced to his left. Oops. Now he'd think I was crazy. Why was Elizabeth so insistent that I tell Pierce about her?

"I guess it was just the wind," he said.

"Yes, probably." I chuckled nervously as I peered up at the still tree branches.

Van wiggled in my arms. I opened the door and placed him inside the Shasta so he could play with his toys. I heard a squeak, indicating he was chewing on his favorite squeaky skunk toy. I closed the door and turned back to the detective.

"Celeste, I appreciate you're trying to help, but you know we're trying to figure it out. We've had a lot of experience with this, not to mention years of training."

He was basically saying I had no experience and shouldn't even bother trying to figure it out. Maybe I'd show him a thing or two about being a detective. Since when did I let a thing like experience get in my way? "I'll keep that in mind," I said.

"Oh, dear. That sounded a bit snippy, don't you think?" Elizabeth asked. "You'll get more flies with honey than vinegar."

"I suppose I should let you get some rest," Pierce said.

I hoped I hadn't upset him.

"Thanks for walking me back," I said. "It is spooky around here at night. Especially with a murder and someone stealing money."

"Just make sure to lock your door. We have an officer patrolling the area," Pierce said.

I raised an eyebrow. "You do?"

"Yes, we do." The corner of his mouth tipped up in a lopsided smile.

"I feel much safer knowing that. By the way, you should smile more often." I pointed at his handsome face.

Even though the dark made it harder to see, I was pretty sure Pierce blushed. His sensual mouth twisted upward on one side. "Good night, Celeste."

"Good night, Detective." My stomach danced as I waved goodbye.

"Why didn't you tell him about me?" Elizabeth waved her arm in a sweeping, dramatic gesture.

"Telling someone you've seen a ghost isn't exactly a casual topic to bring up," I said. "Besides, why did you want him to know so badly?"

Elizabeth followed me into the trailer, where I knew she'd want to continue this conversation.

Elizabeth frowned. "I'm not sure. Something was just telling me that he should know."

"I'll think about telling him, okay?" I pulled down the quilt on the bed.

"It's urgent that you tell him," she said as she leaned against the counter.

"Perhaps you should just show yourself to the detective," I said.

"I don't think it's that easy," she said around a sigh.

CHAPTER 23

Travel trailer tip 23:
Making a checklist might help. Just
don't misplace the list.

Van and I settled into the trailer for the night. If I wanted to read, I usually cozied up in bed, which was exactly what I did tonight. I loved to read about the lives of famous painters, and I was eager to get back to the biography of Van Gogh I had started.

Elizabeth had disappeared. Apparently, she was mad at me. Even though everything was quiet, and I should have been relaxed, my mind wasn't at ease. I kept reading the same paragraph over and over. A heaviness came over the air. I knew what that meant. Within a few seconds, Elizabeth appeared near my kitchenette.

I set down my book. "Where have you been?"

"Just waiting for things to settle down around here so I can talk to you." She glided across the floor. It didn't take long for her to get from one side to the other. I sensed she was still upset. Van watched Elizabeth move back and forth across the trailer too.

"Things have been chaotic around here today," I said.

"I think things have been chaotic since the start of the craft fair." Elizabeth peeked out the window.

"You're right about that."

Van barked in agreement.

"Well, I've been thinking," Elizabeth added, fidgeting with her hands as she moved around the trailer.

"Yes?" I asked.

Van's oversize ears perked up as he waited for her answer.

"I know what might help solve this crime," Elizabeth said.

This was a surprise. Now she had piqued my curiosity. "What?" I asked.

"You need to paint," she said, waving her hand toward my art supplies.

Van barked, as if in complete agreement with her.

"But how will that help me solve the crime?" I asked.

"If you can paint me to life, who knows what or who else you can paint? You should give it a try and see if any clues come forward," she said. "Just think about what happened here and see what comes to you."

"What if I paint someone to life that I really shouldn't? It could be something bad," I said.

"If you worry too much about the what-ifs in life, you'll never do anything," Elizabeth said.

Van tugged on the hem of Elizabeth's floor-length ivory dress with the lace firmly latched in his jaws.

"Van, let go," I said.

Elizabeth reached down to pet Van. Surprisingly, her hand didn't move right through him. He rolled over onto his back for a belly rub.

As she rubbed him, she said, "Well, it certainly can't hurt to try."

"Actually, it possibly could hurt. Like I said, what if I paint something that's bad or scary? What if it brings even more danger? I could bring something evil here."

She raised an eyebrow. "Please reference what I said just a minute ago."

I thought it over. "You know what? Maybe you're right. Maybe I should give it a try."

"If you get a bad feeling, you can stop. After all, I'm here and I'm not bad or evil. Just paint whatever feels right," she said.

"Yes, I guess that would work. I have to do something, right?"

"Absolutely." She clapped her hands. "You should paint right away."

It was kind of late to start a new project tonight, and I was tired. But I was curious at the same time. Plus, I'd painted late into the night before. I retrieved a blank canvas from my stash over in the corner of the trailer. After setting up the easel, I placed the canvas on and spread out my paints. It was a tight fit in this little space, but it was enough.

Sitting in front of the canvas, I studied it, thinking about everything that had happened lately. I hoped something would pop into my head.

It didn't take long before it came to me. I picked

up my brush and dipped it into the green paint. Pressing my brush onto the canvas, I made a long sweep across the white board. I dipped the brush in for more paint and made more strokes. Soon, an image started to appear. I studied the canvas. It was a pine tree. Just a single pine tree on one side of the canvas. But that wasn't all that was in my head. I continued swiping the brush across the blank area, using more colors now.

"It's almost hypnotizing to watch you paint," Elizabeth said from over my shoulder.

I wasn't used to having an audience, so I tried to pretend she wasn't there. The canvas was becoming full with lots of pine and oak trees. Water streamed behind them. It kind of looked like the area surrounding my family's house, with the same tall pines and small creek behind it. What did this have to do with the murder? Was I painting this from memory, or seeing the surroundings of my home in a vision? The painting was beautiful, but it really wasn't anything special.

I had painted Elizabeth, so why couldn't I render an image of who had committed the crime? Something like that had to be possible, I reminded myself. The more I tried, the more frustrated I became. I was losing my confidence now, and that was probably showing through in the strokes on the canvas.

"It's a lovely painting," Elizabeth said, watching over my shoulder. "How will you know when you're finished?"

"Good question. I suppose when the painting is finished."

"How do you know when that happens?" Elizabeth asked.

"I always do," I said, studying what I'd done so far.

"I'm so impressed with your talent," she said.

I smiled. "Thank you, Elizabeth."

Her compliment made me feel a bit better. Before I even realized what I'd done, I had black paint on the tip of my brush, and by the time I had finished, there was a silhouette of a man on the canvas. I gasped in surprise.

"Oh my goodness, it's a man," Elizabeth said.

"What do you think this means?" I asked, looking back at her.

"Could we be looking at the murderer?"

The man's tall height was pronounced on the canvas. Did that mean it was Caleb, Pierce, or Max? They all seemed about the same height. If so, two of the three were already suspects to me, so that didn't narrow it down much. The black paint stood out on the canvas. It seemed as if a shade had been cast across the man's face on purpose, keeping me from capturing his features.

I studied the image, hoping that something else would pop out at me, offering a clue to the man's identity. Pine trees surrounded the craft fair too. Maybe I wasn't trying to paint the area around my house but instead the crime scene here at the craft fair. The man in the silhouette had to be the murderer. Was there a creek nearby and did that hold a clue?

"Maybe that isn't all there is to the painting. Maybe there's more you have to do," Elizabeth said.

I yawned and stretched my arms. "Perhaps, but I think for tonight that is enough. I'm just going to clean up here and sleep. Maybe that will give me time to reenergize. I can try again in the morning."

"That sounds like a lovely idea," Elizabeth said. "So good night, and I'll see you in the morning."

Before I had a chance to say good night or ask where she was going, in the blink of an eye, she was gone. She just disappeared. I wasn't sure how she did it, but there were a lot of things lately I didn't understand. Van barked, as if he was just as stunned as I was.

After cleaning up my brushes, I crawled under the covers. Van curled up against me.

"What would I do without you, my little snuggle buddy?" I asked.

After licking my face, he settled down to sleep. I hoped we both had sweet dreams tonight.

CHAPTER 24

Travel trailer tip 24:
Always lock your door. Check it. Then check it again.

The sun peeked through the slats in the little blinds on the window of my trailer. Morning had arrived and, surprisingly, excitement filled me just thinking about finding out if more ideas for the painting came to me.

After getting up, I went through the routine of giving Van water and food. I had breakfast while reading another chapter of my book. Because cooking was difficult in the trailer, I kept it simple and had a bowl of cereal with a banana.

Van followed me as I moved over to the canvas. I hoped that something would come to me after a night's rest. Elizabeth hadn't shown up yet. I thought I'd see her first thing this morning because she would want to know if I was adding to the painting. Was she busy doing something else? Like what?

After collecting my brushes, I sat down in front of the easel. Brush in hand, I stared at the canvas, but my mind was blank. This was doing no good. I needed to move on to something else.

I didn't know if there was a creek close by, but I planned on checking that out this morning. Now that it was daylight, I would feel much more comfortable about walking around the fair. After all, there were police patrolling the area now. Even though it was the last day, I hoped that meant no one else would be harmed by the murderer.

When I saw my grandmother's phone number pop up on my phone, I knew I had to answer. If I didn't, she'd leave me a message and wonder if something had happened to me. In light of recent events at the fairgrounds, she would think I had been murdered.

When I answered, she said, "What are you doing? I thought you weren't going to answer. I thought you'd been murdered."

"It only rang three times, Grandma," I said.

"Well, that's two times too many. I was worried sick about you."

"Is everything all right, Grandma?" I asked.

"Oh, everything is just peachy with me," she said. "Speaking of peaches, I've been canning some today. I need you to come out to pick them up."

"I can swing by later."

"Swing by? There is no swinging by your grandmother's house. That simply doesn't happen." This was an urgent matter for her, so I knew I'd better not wait too long.

"Grandma, I would love to talk more, but I have to get back to work." She didn't need to know what that work involved at the moment.

"Do you have customers already?" she asked.

"Well, not customers per se, but I think I see some people coming."

"Well, if you must go." The sound of shuffling papers sounded through the other end of the line. "But there is one other thing I called about."

"What's that?" I paced across the floor while Van watched me.

"I need you to come by to look at an old photo album."

"Why is that?" I asked as I checked the time. This didn't seem like such an urgent matter. I knew she just wanted to spend time with me. I loved spending time with her too. She told the most amazing stories.

"I have a picture I think you might be interested in seeing."

"Okay, well, like I said, I can come by later and you can show it to me."

"You really need to see this right away," she said.

"Okay, I can come by later this afternoon. I could ask Sammie to come by to watch the booth for me."

"That would be a great idea," she said. "You know, even better yet, I'll just come to you right now. I'll bring the album and the peaches. Now, don't make a habit of not coming to visit your grandma. And having me bring you things."

"I don't want you to do that, Grandma. I can come by there."

"No, no. This is urgent, and I want to come by now."

"Are you sure it's not an emergency? Should I call Mom and have her come over?"

"No, no. This is just something I want to talk to you about," she said.

"If you insist," I said.

"I'll be there in a jiffy."

Grandma hung up the phone, leaving me confused. What was so urgent that she needed to see me right away? Now I had to wait until she arrived. I stepped outside to enjoy the cooler morning air before the heat arrived. I kept looking at my watch, wondering when Grandma would arrive. The wait was making me nervous. I didn't like for her to drive, but she'd insisted. I hoped I was as lively as her at the age of eighty-five.

A few minutes later, when I looked to my left, I spotted Grandma headed down the path toward me. She marched in my direction as if she was on a mission. This must be serious. I smiled at the sight of her. She wore her pink Capri pants and white blouse with her pink sandals that had big flowers on the tops. She'd even added her pink lipstick and had her straw pocketbook looped on her arm. On the other arm she was caring a big photo album. I waved and motioned for her to come over.

When she stopped in front of me, she plopped the leather album down on the table.

I squeezed her in a hug. "I'm glad you're here, Grandma."

"Not so tight," she said.

"It was a long walk over here for you, I suppose."

She waved her hand. "Oh, it wasn't that far. Quit worrying about me. I'm healthy and I can walk. As long as I have legs that work, I'm using them. There are too many people who can't get around, so I don't want to complain when I can move just fine."

"Yes, Grandma," I said.

This wasn't the first time I'd gotten this talk. I needed to remember not to persuade her to sit when she didn't want to.

She opened up the album, flipped to the middle, and pointed to a picture in the middle of the page. "Do you recognize this woman?"

I almost fell over onto the ground. "Yes, I recognize her."

"That's why I said you had to see this."

"Where did you get this photo?"

It was almost identical to the painting I'd done of Elizabeth. So I'd seen this photo before, obviously. That was why I'd painted it. I'd gotten the image from the back of my mind. It was always there. But I didn't know her.

"Why do you have a photo of Elizabeth?"

"This is your great-great-great-aunt," she said.

"You're kidding me. All this time she was related to me and we didn't know it? Didn't you recognize her name?" I asked.

"Well, no, because I think she gave you her maiden name. And I only know her as Maurice, which was her married name. But I started thinking about it more, and that's what made me get out the album. And when I saw the picture, I thought it sounded exactly the way you described her."

"Yes, let me show you the painting." I rushed over and pulled it out from the trailer.

My grandmother stood back and studied the

canvas while comparing it to the photo. "Uncanny. Are you going to tell her? Is she here now?"

"She's not here now. I'll definitely tell her when I see her."

My grandmother closed the album. "Well, I should let you get to work. I suppose people will be here soon."

I crossed my fingers. "I hope so."

She kissed my cheek. "Good luck."

"What about the peaches?" I asked.

She wiggled her finger. "I left them at home. I know how to get you to come by for a visit."

"I'll be by soon to get them." I smiled.

As she headed off down the path, I called out, "Please drive carefully."

Now that Grandma had gone, I had to go for my walk. Leaving Van in the trailer, I headed down the path. I went toward the area with the most trees. Even though we were close to town, the fairgrounds were on the edge and had some natural setting all around.

The sun had already warmed things up and I knew it would be another hot day. Even if I found a creek nearby, I figured I probably wouldn't find any clues, but there had to be a reason why the scene was in the painting. I'd try my best to figure it out.

The farther I walked through the wooded area, the more apprehensive I became. I just wanted to get a quick look to see for myself. I had to know if there was any truth to this painting.

Almost as soon as I walked into the wooded area, I spotted the creek. So this really was what I'd painted. It was the fairgrounds after all. Now I had to figure out who the man was and how he'd come to the creek. What could tie this location to the murder?

It was quiet here, except for the gentle sound of the water flowing over the rocks. The sound of traffic in the distance broke through, and I heard faint voices from the fairgrounds. Even though people were close by, I couldn't help but realize the creepiness of the secluded setting.

A crunching and snapping noise came from somewhere over my shoulder. It sounded as if someone had stepped on a fallen branch. I whipped around. No one was there. Thank goodness for that. It must've been a squirrel.

After a few more seconds of looking around, I turned my attention back to the creek. It was just a couple of inches deep, with clear water showing the pebbles at its bottom, just as I had painted it. At least I knew my painting was right. I headed away from the creek, happy that I had visited. Maybe something else would come to mind and I could paint that as well.

As I walked away, a strange feeling came over me. I sensed that someone was around, as if I was about to have a visitor. I scanned the area. I just hoped that if someone popped up, it wasn't an unwelcome visitor . . . like the murderer.

The sun hadn't fully appeared yet. Streaks of red and orange filled the blue eastern sky. Was someone hiding from me? I walked again, hurrying my steps so that I could get away from the treed area. Movement caught my attention. When I looked to the left, I noticed a woman looking around as if she was searching for someone.

Shocked, I recognized Madame Gerard and had a feeling she was searching for me.

I rushed over to the psychic. "Madame Gerard, what are you doing here?"

"I've been looking for you," she said. "I'm glad I found you."

Well, it was more like I'd found her, but I supposed we'd found each other. This must be serious if she'd tracked me down.

"Is something wrong?" I asked.

"A spirit came through to me and he wants to speak with you. He said you painted him, but I don't know what that means. He's bad and I don't like speaking with him. I brought him here to you," she said with a wave of her hand.

If he was bad, I was so grateful she'd brought him over here to me. I mean that in the most sarcastic way possible. She should've just told him to get lost.

"Can't you tell him to go away?"

"It doesn't work that way. I don't want to talk to bad spirits," she said.

This was what I've been afraid of: that I would bring through something that wasn't so nice. I looked around but didn't see a spirit.

"Why did you bring him with you?" I asked.

"I'm here to deliver the message. If he came with me, there's nothing I can do about that. I just want him away from me."

"I painted his image, but it wasn't on purpose. I'm supposed to volunteer to take him? If he's with you, there's not much I can do to make him leave you alone," I said. Finders keepers, right?

"You can stop painting things and bringing them to me," she said.

I supposed that meant she didn't want me to come around anymore.

She looked around to the left and then to the right. "There's danger all around here."

Well, I didn't need a psychic to tell me that. After all, there had been a murder.

"There's someone else watching you."

"Other than the bad person? Maybe it's a nice person, as in someone's watching over me." I attempted a grin.

"Yes, you could say that," she said.

"Is her name Elizabeth?"

"I don't know. I'm not getting that information."

"Is there any other information you are getting?" I asked. "I need to know everything I possibly can. This is very important."

"I understand the importance. That's why I came to find you," she said.

"I really appreciate that," I said.

She frowned in concentration, as if someone was talking to her. I waited anxiously for the response.

"The person who is watching you. It's a secret."

"What kind of secret?" I asked.

"I don't know," Madame Gerard said. "This is incredibly frustrating."

She was giving me hints at things, and now I had to try to figure out what they meant.

"Don't you have any other clues you can offer me?" I asked.

She once again looked around. "I think the person is watching us right now."

That sent a shiver down my spine. I looked around the area as well, hoping to spot this mystery person. I saw no one. Whoever was hiding was really good at it.

"Maybe I should just go back into my trailer," I said.

The psychic rubbed her arms, as if fighting off a chill. "I think I should get out of here too before something else happens."

She turned around and headed around one of the pine trees. When she was out of sight, I rushed back out to the path. I didn't want to be alone anymore.

I bolted back into the trailer and locked the door behind me. Van barked, letting me know he wanted breakfast. He probably also wanted to know where I'd been.

"There's someone bad out there, Van."

I went over to the window and peeked outside. How long would the person watch?

CHAPTER 25

Travel trailer tip 25:
Secure your doors and windows, and close the shade
when you're away. Don't forget where you put the keys.

After a change of clothing, I left my little trailer behind at the craft fair as I pointed the truck in the direction of Madame Gerard's house. She had left me with unanswered questions, and I intended to get those answers.

Elizabeth sat in the passenger seat, with Van in the middle between us. At least I wasn't alone for this trip. I needed another person with me. Although I wasn't quite sure anyone else could see Elizabeth sitting in the truck, I knew she was there, and that was all that mattered right now.

Now was as good a time as any to tell Elizabeth that we were related. I hoped she would be just as excited with the news as I was.

"I discovered something this morning," I said.

"Oh, a clue to find the murderer?" Elizabeth asked excitedly.

"No, this is different."

Elizabeth frowned. "I hope it's not bad."

"Actually, I think it's good." I stopped at a red light.

"Now I'm curious."

"You're my great-great-great-aunt."

She scrunched her brow. "Your great-great-great-aunt? How do you know that?"

"My grandmother found your picture in her photo album."

Elizabeth smiled. "Honest? How exciting. I can't tell you how happy this makes me. That explains why you painted me. I obviously came back here to help because there was going to be danger at the craft fair."

"Fate has things worked out." The light turned green and I took off.

"I want to see the photo," she said.

"As soon as the craft fair is over, I'll take you to my grandmother's."

Elizabeth grinned. "I'd like that."

"Should I call you Aunt Elizabeth?"

"I'd like that even more," she said.

"Do you think anyone else sees you?" I asked as I steered the truck.

"I'm not sure," Elizabeth said. "Your friend can see me. Maybe only a select few get the lucky advantage of knowing me."

I chuckled. "Yes, maybe it's just certain people."

"I think it's probably certain people who have a sixth sense." Elizabeth tapped her index finger against her temple.

"I'm curious to know if the psychic will be able to see you." I traveled through a green light. "She sees other spirits, so why not you too?"

"Well, that is her job," Elizabeth said. "I certainly won't hide from her on purpose."

"I guess we'll find out."

I made a left turn and after a few more blocks, we reached Madame Gerard's house. I was kind of nervous about seeing her again. What would she have to say this time? I hoped it wasn't more bad news.

After parking the truck, I picked up Van. I grabbed my bag with my other hand and headed toward the psychic's front door. Elizabeth was walking along beside us. I wondered if Madame Gerard would be surprised to see me so soon. Probably no more surprised than I'd been to see her at the craft fair. Plus, I'd brought a special spirit friend along.

Once at the front door, I released a deep breath and pushed the button to ring her. I waited for any sign that she was home. The "Open" sign cast its eerie glow over the entire area. I hoped she was really here. Maybe she was ignoring me. A thickness lingered in the air, but I assumed it was the usual humidity. I hoped it was nothing more sinister. It was probably just my nerves, I reminded myself.

A shuffling noise came from the other side of the door. Madame Gerard peeked out through the blinds, just as she had the last time. Her dazzling blue eyes practically glowed as she watched me.

I knew she recognized me. The blinds closed

and there was no other sound. Was she going to ignore me, act as if I wasn't there? Now I felt kind of foolish for coming back. Maybe she was just strange and there had never been a spirit talking to her. She probably hadn't meant for me to return.

Elizabeth said, "Do you think she's going to let you in?"

"I hope so, but now I'm beginning to wonder. Maybe this was a bad idea," I said.

A familiar sound came from the other side of the door. The locks. She was going through each one. Elizabeth stepped back, as if she was unsure what the psychic would do next. Finally, Madame Gerard opened the door just a crack. She eyed me up and down.

"Remember me?" I asked. "My name is Celeste Cabot. You came to see me this morning."

Instantly, her attention fixed on Elizabeth. "You brought another ghost with you?"

Wow. It hadn't taken her long to notice.

"Yes. I hope you don't mind. I don't mean any harm," I said.

She opened the door wider. "Please come in."

Madame Gerard saw Elizabeth too. This was exciting. Now I wanted to know if she could tell me more about Aunt Elizabeth. Perhaps the psychic would have details Elizabeth didn't remember. That might seem crazy, but anything was possible at this point. Elizabeth and I entered the house and went to the right, into the room Madame Gerard had pointed out.

"Please have a seat at the table." The bangle bracelets on her wrists jingled when she motioned.

Candles flickered around the room. Madame Gerard's crystal ball was in the middle of the table. I peered into the glass, wondering if I would actually see anything. Did I have psychic ability? I wasn't sure. But I knew I saw Elizabeth. So had Sammie and Madame Gerard.

Elizabeth followed me into the room. I sat down in the same chair as before, and Elizabeth took a seat in the chair where Sammie had sat. It was a neat trick that Elizabeth could actually sit in the chair. She did everything a living person could do and even more. Van sat next to me on the other side. He acted as if he knew exactly why we were there.

Madame Gerard took her place across from us. She hadn't mentioned if the bad spirit was still around. I hoped he had gone. Madame Gerard's attention turned to Elizabeth. She looked surprised to see a ghost here. I figured she must have experienced quite a few ghosts, considering her profession. Maybe no one had ever brought a ghost with them.

"She wasn't with you when you were here last," Madame Gerard pointed out.

Elizabeth fidgeted in the seat. Obviously, Madame Gerard's stare made her uncomfortable.

Madame Gerard stretched out her arms toward us. "Let's all hold hands."

When I tried to hold Elizabeth's hand, mine went right through hers. Was she fading? Her energy didn't seem as strong.

Madame Gerard chuckled. "Sorry, I suppose I forgot."

"It will be impossible for us to hold hands with Elizabeth," I said.

"This is the first time I've had an actual ghost sitting at the table like this," Madame Gerard said.

"Really?" I asked with a frown. "I would've thought it would happen all the time. As a matter of fact, I thought when I was here you saw the ghost who was talking to you. I thought you saw the spirit with you this morning. But you couldn't see the ghost?"

"No, that's not the way it works for me," Madame Gerard said. "I just see them in my mind. I've never seen a ghost in person."

Again, Madame Gerard stared at Elizabeth.

"Well, I suppose there's a first for everything," I said.

"I'm surprised you came back so soon."

"I thought maybe it was necessary. After what you said, I have questions." I motioned with a tilt of my head toward Elizabeth.

"I don't think I have the answers you want." Madame Gerard attempted a smile. That was the first time I'd actually seen her smile. "Take my hand, and we'll just pretend we're holding Elizabeth's hands." Madame Gerard wiggled her fingers.

"What will I do?" Elizabeth asked.

"You can use your mind to concentrate with us." The psychic closed her eyes.

Again, I opened one eye and peeked around the room to see if another ghost popped up. I wanted to know who Madame Gerard had been talking with before. If the ghost returned, maybe I could see it.

"Okay. There is another ghost here," Madame Gerard said.

With both my eyes open now, I saw no sign of a ghost. The spirit was just appearing in Madame Gerard's mind.

CHAPTER 26

Travel trailer tip 26:
Befriend your neighbors, even the ones who
aren't so nice. You'll enjoy the nice ones. And
you'll be able to keep an eye on the others.

I waited anxiously for Madame Gerard to say something.

Elizabeth and Van both had their eyes closed. Okay, Van was lying on the chair sleeping, but still, he had his eyes closed. Maybe he knew what we were doing.

"I call to the spirits," Madame Gerard said. Her eyes were still closed. Of course I was peeking. "Who wants to speak with Celeste?" she said. "Anyone? Anyone? Now is the time to come forward."

She opened her eyes and peered into the crystal ball. She hadn't looked at me to notice that my eyes were open too. I wasn't sure if I was supposed to do that or not. But I was looking into that crystal ball as well. I hoped to see someone I recognized.

Would the spirit be able to manifest outside the

crystal ball and come into the room? Would the spirit sit down with us at the table, just like Elizabeth? It could get awfully crowded in here if that happened. Madame Gerard would need more chairs. Madame Gerard scrunched her brow in concentration as she stared at the glass ball. I saw absolutely nothing in there, but it seemed as if she was looking at something.

"Oh spirits, come forward. We ask you to give us a message for Celeste," Madame Gerard said.

This was spooky. I wasn't sure if I actually wanted another spirit to come through.

"I know you're around. I can sense you," she said.

I looked around the room but saw nothing unusual. Elizabeth had opened her eyes at this point, but Madame Gerard still hadn't looked at either of us. I supposed she was in her trance and concentrating on the spirits who had arrived. They weren't speaking yet.

"I'm having a bit of a problem hearing or understanding the spirit right now. We'll continue, and hopefully it will become clearer now."

Perhaps she needed to fine tune the crystal ball for better reception. Maybe the spirits were just being difficult. Madame Gerard released our hands and jumped up from the table. What was going on?

"I'll be right back," she said as she stood. "Don't move."

Now I was really scared. But I didn't move. I looked over to make sure Van was all right. He was sleeping. Whatever was going on, he didn't seem bothered by it. Madame Gerard walked out of the room and disappeared into what I assumed was the kitchen.

"What's going on?" Elizabeth asked.

"I don't know, but it's making me anxious," I whispered.

"Me too," she said. "Maybe we should just leave."

"Madame Gerard said we shouldn't go anywhere and that we shouldn't move. I'm thinking she said that for a reason."

"Yes, but maybe that reason was bad," Elizabeth said.

A few more seconds went by before Madame Gerard emerged into the room again. She held a glass bowl. Whatever was in the bowl, she used it to sprinkle around the room. It looked like salt. As she moved around the room, she didn't speak to us. I had to know what she was doing.

"Is that salt?" I asked.

"It's to keep out the bad spirits." She pinched more salt between her index finger and her thumb.

Oh no. I was afraid of that. Had bad spirits been trying to communicate?

"Should I be worried?" My voice wavered.

"Well, it's common for bad things to come. I told you this morning I didn't like speaking with them. We just have to take precautions," she said. "That's what I'm doing right now. Try not to worry too much."

She didn't sound all that confident, so that wasn't reassuring. Nevertheless, I tried to remain calm and not completely freak out.

After Madame Gerard had gone around the entire perimeter of the room, she came back over to the table and put the bowl down. She motioned for us to give our hands back to her. She chuckled. "I forgot again."

I held Madame Gerard's hand again and pretended to hold Elizabeth's hand.

"Now we can continue," Madame Gerard said. "We'll just say a little safety spell when we're finished."

I had a feeling there was something she wasn't telling me. That there was something negative lingering around and she was worried about it. Nevertheless, Madame Gerard started over. "I call to the spirits. I know you're here. I can see you. Reveal yourself now, and your message," she said.

We waited for another long pause, possibly for an answer to arrive. The longer this took, the more I thought maybe we should just give up on it.

"The spirit is showing me the painting. The one I told you about this morning. There are pine trees surrounding a silhouette of a man. Do you know this location? Or what the spirit might be trying to tell me?" Madame Gerard asked. "Could it be the area by the creek?"

"I just painted that last night and this morning," I said excitedly. "I think the silhouette is the man who murdered Evan. And yes, it was by the creek where you found me. Max's trailer and the office for the fairgrounds are close to that creek."

Madame Gerard opened her eyes. "There has been a murder. The one at the craft fair?"

"Yes, that's right," I said.

"I heard about that," she said. "As I said before, this is something dark."

Out of nowhere, Elizabeth said, "I think I recognize the man in the silhouette. I'm almost certain it's Max. I can see Evan in the room with us. He's bad, but that's just because he was so rude when he was alive. He says he means us no harm."

"How do you know that? Just because he says it doesn't make it true," I said.

"I'm just repeating what he said," Elizabeth said.

"Is that what you hear too?" I looked at Madame Gerard.

"Yes, he says Max murdered him. The spirit is Evan."

"Wow, you're talking with the spirit of Evan?" I asked.

Madame Gerard shook her head. "He didn't tell me his name."

"It is Evan," Elizabeth said.

"What does this man look like?" I asked.

"He's a large man with gray sprinkled in his dark hair," Elizabeth said as she pointed toward her head.

That could be Evan.

"We have to get the police right away," I said, jumping up from my chair.

"What are you going to tell them?" Elizabeth asked. "That a ghost and a psychic told you to do this?"

I sat back down. "You're right. What am I going to tell them? I wish the detective could see you too. Why can't he see you?"

"I can't make people see me if they don't," Elizabeth said.

"Yes, I suppose that's true. Maybe he just needs to open his mind to the paranormal and he would be able to see you."

"That's easier said than done," Madame Gerard

said. "It takes a while sometimes for people to realize the paranormal is out there."

"Maybe there's something I can do to push him in that direction. But in the meantime, Max could be plotting another murder. I don't think I have enough time for that. I'll have to find a way to tell Pierce and get him to believe me. If only we could get Max to confess," I said.

"I highly doubt that would happen," Elizabeth said.

"No, usually people don't confess to murder," Madame Gerard said.

Van barked, as if he was agreeing with us.

"We have to go," I said as I stood from my chair.

"Wait. There is one other thing." Madame Gerard touched my arm.

"What's that?" I asked.

"There was something else I saw in the crystal ball." She focused her attention on Elizabeth.

"Is it about me?" Elizabeth asked.

"There's a connection between you two." Madame Gerard pointed from Elizabeth to me. "Kindred spirits, perhaps?"

"My grandmother found a photo of Elizabeth. It turns out, she is my great-great-great-aunt," I said.

"That explains a lot," Madame Gerard said.

"I can tell you more about it later. Right now, we need to get to the fairgrounds," I said.

"Please be careful," Madame Gerard said. "I think you're going into a very dangerous situation."

Did she know more that she wasn't telling me? Elizabeth, Van, and I rushed out of Madame Gerard's house. As soon as I got into the truck, I pulled out my phone.

"I was going to suggest that you use that little contraption to call the detective," Elizabeth said.

Unfortunately, Pierce didn't answer, so I had to leave a message. "I think Max is the killer, and I think he's planning to kill someone else. Call me immediately. I'm going to stop him." I rushed my words. I knew I sounded panicked. That was because I *was* panicked.

"I'm not sure he'll understand what you were saying. Don't forget to breathe," Elizabeth said.

"Right." I cranked the engine.

Trying not to speed, I pointed the truck in the direction of the craft fair.

"I hope it's not too late," I said. "What if he's already got another victim?"

"Oh, dear. I certainly hope not too," Elizabeth said.

I punched the gas when the light turned yellow so I wouldn't have to stop.

Once we arrived back at the fairgrounds, I parked the truck next to my trailer and shut off the engine. "We have to find Max."

"This is very dangerous, Celeste," Elizabeth said. "If he discovers you know about what he's done, he could make you his next victim."

"I know, but if he does something to someone else and I had a chance to stop it, I'll feel really bad. I'd never forgive myself."

"Maybe you should call Caleb and have him meet you. Then the two of you can find Max together. I would feel much better if you had someone with you."

"I hate to put him in danger too," I said.

"Max won't be able to do something to both of

you. It would be better if you don't go alone. I'm adamant about this," Elizabeth said.

I pulled out my phone. "Okay, I'll give him a call, but we don't have much time."

Unfortunately, Caleb didn't answer his phone. I left him a voice mail anyway, and told him it was urgent. I didn't say what I wanted to talk to him about because I didn't want him to look for Max on his own. That was too dangerous. Sure, Caleb would want to know why I thought it was too dangerous for him but perfectly fine for me. I didn't have an answer for that. I just hoped Caleb wasn't anywhere near Max. For that matter, I hoped no one was near him.

After placing the call to Caleb, I dialed Pierce again. He didn't answer this time either. Where was everyone today? I left another message for Pierce too. I told him it was urgent that he meet me at my trailer. It was a matter of life or death. That was the truth as far as I was concerned. Max could strike again at any time.

"Maybe I should go to Caleb's trailer," I said.

"Good idea," Elizabeth said.

"It'll be faster if I drive over there." I turned the engine and backed away from my trailer.

"Another good idea," Elizabeth said.

Once by Caleb's booth, I found a spot to park next to a treed area. Anxiety danced in my stomach as I got out of the truck and hurried over to his trailer.

"I hope he's here," Elizabeth said.

"Me too," I said.

Van barked as I held him in my arms. He was

agreeing with me. So far, there was no sign of Caleb or Gum Shoe.

"He could be anywhere," I said.

As I stood at the trailer door and knocked, I shifted from foot to foot. After a few seconds with no answer, I was ready to give up and go find Max.

"He's not here. I just have to hope he's okay."

He hadn't answered the text I'd sent. Of course, I'd been vague with my message. I didn't want to come right out and say that Max was the killer until I knew for sure. Though maybe I should hint at it so Caleb could be safe from him.

"He's not here, so I'll just have to go back over to my trailer. I'll park the truck and start searching for Max. And maybe in the meantime, Caleb will show up," I said.

"That's the only plan we have," Elizabeth said.

"Well, it's the only plan I can come up with," I said.

"It'll have to do," she said.

As I headed back over to my truck, my phone rang. It was Caleb's number.

"Oh, thank goodness it's him," I said.

"I'm so relieved," Elizabeth said.

When I answered the call, I said, "Caleb, I need to see you right away."

There was no response.

"Hello?" I said.

Still, there was no answer. When I peered down at my phone, I realized the call had been dropped. Without giving it a second thought, I dialed his number again. After just a few rings, it went to his voice mail. That made me nervous all over again. What if he was trying to reach me for help?

"The call was dropped," I said.

"What does that mean?" Elizabeth asked.

"It means the signal was lost."

"Signal lost," she said, as if she really didn't understand but was acknowledging me.

"What if Max has already found him?" I asked.

"Try not to think the worst," Elizabeth said.

I would try, but it wouldn't be easy. I sent Caleb another text, telling him that it was urgent that I speak with him. I just hoped he was able to respond soon so I could stop worrying. I wouldn't stop until I knew he was safe, and that Max couldn't harm anyone else.

I had to tell Caleb that Max was bad. I had to warn him. It just wouldn't be right if I didn't give him a bit of a heads-up.

By the way, Max . . . stay away from him. I'll explain later. Just avoid him at all cost.

"That should make you feel somewhat better," Elizabeth said.

"Not really," I said.

"What are we doing now?" Elizabeth asked.

"We need to find Max quickly. Plus, I hope the detective is here soon," I said as I pulled up to my trailer again.

I jumped out of the truck and hurried around the side of my Shasta. I was immediately stopped when Ruth stepped in front of me. I didn't have time to talk to her right now. She seemed a bit out of sorts. Her normally shiny brown hair appeared a bit tousled and her navy-blue embroidered blouse and white-linen, ankle-length skirt were wrinkled.

"Excuse me," I said, trying to move around her.

"Where do you think you're going?" Ruth asked.

She narrowed her eyes and glared at me. Her lip curled to one side, as if she was actually snarling at me.

She was being rude, so I asked, "Why do you want to know?" My tone was a bit snippy, but I didn't like the way she was staring at me. Unfortunately, she didn't answer. I noticed she was looking at someone behind me. Did she see Elizabeth? When I looked to my left, I realized Elizabeth was standing right next to me. So Ruth couldn't be watching her.

When I glanced over my shoulder, I spotted Max. This was not how I had hoped this would turn out. I wanted to be the one in charge of this encounter. Not to be confronted. Now, it looked as if I was trapped between the two of them. Ruth seemed ready to lunge after me. Max remained expressionless, which was even more disturbing than if he'd snarled or growled at me. If I didn't know better, I'd say Ruth was helping him.

Panic had taken over my body. If Ruth wasn't involved with Max, I had to warn her so she could run as well. It seemed as if running might be my only way to get away. When I turned around to look at Max, he was giving me the evilest look I had ever seen.

"What do you want?" I asked.

"I think you should mind your own business," Max said.

It was too late for that. "I know what you've done," I said.

"Maybe you shouldn't have told him that," Elizabeth said. "You should've left him guessing."

"I think he already knew anyway," I said, glancing at Elizabeth.

Yes, I was talking to Elizabeth, and Max gave a confused look. He wasn't sure who I was talking to or if I'd totally lost it.

"Ruth, you should get out of here," I yelled.

Checking over my shoulder, I realized Ruth was still glaring at me. Well, that explained why she'd jumped out in front of me. She was working with Max. I would never have guessed the two of them were in cahoots.

"You've been taking the money and giving it to Max, right?" I asked. "You were working together."

"How clever you are," Ruth said.

"And you killed Evan," I said.

"Right again," Max said with a click of his tongue.

"This is scaring me, Celeste," Elizabeth said. "You have to get out of here."

With Ruth behind me and Max in front, I wasn't sure how escaping would be possible. I was trapped, with nowhere to go. I supposed there wasn't a way to talk myself out of the situation either.

"Why did you do this?" I asked.

"That's not something I can discuss with you," Max said.

"You wanted Evan's job," I said. "And Ruth, I'm not sure why you did this. You just wanted the money, I guess."

That was when it hit me. I remembered what I'd seen in her trailer. The name on the paper gave away Ruth's real identity.

"You're Max's mother," I said. "And that's why you're doing this. You two are in on this together to take everyone's money. Ruth Stone. That's your real name, not Ruth Gordon. You're Max's mother!"

"I'm a proud mama," she said, holding her head high.

"Evan found out about what you were doing," I said. "It all makes sense now."

"You are a clever one," Ruth said with a wiggle of her finger. "I knew we would have trouble out of you when I saw those paintings. Such talent. It's too bad that now it'll all be over for you."

I didn't like the way that sounded. Did she mean it would all be over as in no more painting, or were they going to murder me? I probably knew the answer to my question.

"Oh, Celeste, you have to get away from them," Elizabeth said.

I tried to remain calm and contemplate my options. Which were few. I could try to run past Max, but he would just reach out and grab me. Or I could move back and run past his mother. I was pretty sure the same scenario would play out with that option.

If only I could cause a distraction, I'd run. But once they figured out it was just a distraction, they would come after me. I had my phone in my pocket. If I could dial 911, maybe I could get a bit of help.

Was there any other way to defend myself? They could just kill me right here and no one would see. That was exactly what they'd done to Evan. And that was probably what they intended for me.

Ruth pulled out a carving knife from her pocket.

Although it was small, I knew it could cause a fatal injury. Van bared his teeth and growled.

"Another carving knife to the neck? Is that what you're going to do? Can't you be more original than that?" I shielded Van with my arms to protect him in case she made a move.

"Pardon me for interrupting, Celeste, but perhaps you shouldn't antagonize them," Elizabeth said. "They're already angry."

I totally saw her point. However, if they were angry, that might mean their minds weren't as clear and their thinking would be skewed. Their logic would be gone, and I would be able to out-smart them. It was the only plan I could think of.

"Don't worry, we have something completely different in store for you," Ruth said with an evil grin. "Don't you want to find out what it is?"

"Not particularly, no," I said. "You won't get away with this. I've already contacted the police and they're on their way."

"Don't listen to her, Max. She's just saying that. It's not true," Ruth said.

Max looked as if he was contemplating the idea. I had put doubt in his mind. He didn't know if I had called the cops or not.

"Oh, I most definitely called," I said. "And they should be here any second."

CHAPTER 27

Travel tip number 27:
Sometimes it takes a bit to get the hang of things.

Placing Van on the ground, I lunged forward, running toward Max. Maybe he would be so surprised, it would throw him off his guard. As fast as my legs would allow, I ran for him. His eyes widened when he realized what was happening. Stretching his arms out, he readied himself to tackle me.

When I was almost upon him, I darted to the left to dodge around him. Unfortunately, my calculations were off, and Max managed to grab me. We tumbled to the ground. The weight of his body almost crushed me. I was more concerned about Van. I could hear him barking. When I looked to the left, I realized he'd taken off. That was my worst nightmare. I would never be able to find him now—though that might not matter, because it looked as if Max was going to kill me right there by my trailer.

"Hurry up and get rid of her before someone sees us," Ruth said.

"Oh, Celeste, how are you going to get out of this?" Elizabeth asked.

Max was dragging me away from the trailer and trying to get me in his car. But I wouldn't go without a fight. I knew once he got me in the vehicle, it would be all over for me. I would stand a better chance of getting away if I were here. Maybe someone would hear all the commotion.

Ruth raced over and grabbed my leg. Max was pulling me from the upper body. The next thing I knew, loud, growling sounds surrounded us. Ruth screamed. She was shaking her leg, trying to get Van to release his grip on her. His teeth had pierced her ankle. Van wasn't alone. He had brought reinforcements.

Caleb's German shepherd, Gum Shoe, stood over Ruth now, growling and baring his teeth. Van released his hold and Ruth froze on the spot. Max let go of me, obviously afraid the dog would attack his mother.

I pushed to my feet and raced over to grab Van.

"Gum Shoe, where are you?" Caleb yelled.

As I raced around the trailer, I smacked right into him.

"Are you all right, Celeste?" he asked.

He looked over my shoulder and spotted Gum Shoe standing over Ruth and Max, who were both frozen in fear.

"Don't stop him," I said. "You have to call the police. Max is the killer and Ruth is his accomplice. She's also his mom! They were trying to kidnap me to murder me. Thank goodness Van and Gum Shoe stopped them."

Caleb was ready to pull out his phone when police cars surrounded us.

"Put your hands up," an officer said as he jumped out of his car.

We all did as we were told. I put one hand up because I was holding Van with my other one. I was surprised that neither Max nor Ruth had tried to run. I supposed they knew when it was over for them.

Now I had to explain to the police officers what had happened, and they needed to place Max and Ruth in handcuffs. About twenty police cars had descended on the area.

Caleb got Gum Shoe and patted his head. "Good job, buddy. He took off with Van. I didn't know what was going on, so I followed them."

"I can't believe Van went to get his buddy to save me. Van is my hero. And Gum Shoe too. I don't know what I would've done without them."

"They're brave," Caleb said.

As we stood behind my Shasta near the old oak tree, I looked around for Elizabeth, but she was nowhere to be found.

"Are you looking for someone?" Caleb asked as he rubbed Van's head.

I sighed. "No."

What was the point? He couldn't see her anyway. Sunlight filtered through the tree's branches splashing across Caleb's handsome face and blond-streaked hair. The tall trees creaked and the leaves rustled in the wind.

"I have something to confess," I said.

"Is that right? What is it?" Caleb asked as he swatted away a mosquito.

"You were on the top of my suspects list. I mean, no offense, but you were right there when Evan was killed. You had those cuts on your hands, and I saw you with all that money. Not to mention the bloody shirt."

"You saw the shirt, huh? I suppose that looked suspicious. I just didn't want you to know how clumsy I am."

"I'd rather have known you were clumsy than think you were the killer," I said.

"Yet you still went out with me?" he asked.

"I figured if I went out with you, I could get closer, and maybe get some clues. Or a confession."

"That was very dangerous, Celeste," he said.

"That's what I told her," Elizabeth said.

I jumped when I realized she was beside me again.

"Anyway, like I said, I didn't want to believe it."

"You didn't?" Caleb asked.

"No, I didn't. Well, you're so nice," I said.

"I try to be," he said while blushing.

"So what about the cuts on your hands?" I leaned against the oak tree's trunk to step out of the sunshine.

"It was exactly like I told you," he said.

"Well, you said a couple of things, one to Aunt Patsy and another to me."

"They were both true," he said.

"I should apologize for thinking you were the killer and had stolen all that money."

"I suppose I should say the same to you," he said.

"You really thought I was the killer? That I was capable of doing something like that?"

"In my line of work, I have to be suspicious of everyone. No matter how nice they seem, the person could always be hiding something."

"That's true. I won't hold that against you."

He laughed. "Thank you. I'm just glad we have the perpetrators now.

"Maybe things will get back to normal," I said.

"Speaking of normal, do you plan on going to the Farewell Summer Arts and Crafts Fair in a couple of weeks? It's over in Cherokee."

I smiled. "Yes, I plan on going. What about you?"

"I think it would be a good idea," he said. "I had a lot of fun hanging around with you. And I'd like to continue that now that this fair is almost over."

I knew I was probably blushing. Speaking of blushing, Pierce had arrived and was speaking with another detective. I didn't think they'd even noticed me yet. The way I felt about spending more time with Caleb, I also felt about Pierce. What would I do? I wouldn't tell Caleb about my feelings, that was for sure.

As if on cue, Pierce waved. Caleb noticed him and tossed up his hand.

"Wait a minute. You're not enemies?" I asked. "It seemed like you two didn't like each other."

"Well, I wouldn't say enemies, no."

"The tension is definitely there when you two are around each other," I said.

"I suppose we have our reasons," he said.

"What are those reasons?" I eyed him suspiciously.

"I'm not sure I can disclose that right now," Caleb said.

Why couldn't he just give me an honest answer? Why were things so secretive? Wait. Madame Gerard said someone was watching me and it was a secret.

"You knew each other before meeting here, didn't you? And what did you mean when you said in your line of work, you have to be suspicious of everyone? You don't mean being a wood sculptor, do you?"

"I was wondering when you were going to catch that," he said with a sheepish grin.

"The stress slowed me down, I guess. Are you going to tell me what's going on here?" I asked.

"I'm a detective with the police department. I've been working undercover. We knew someone had been taking money from craft fairs."

"Your real name is Caleb Ward, though, right?"

"Yes, my name is Caleb Ward. And I am a wood sculptor. Maybe not a great one, but I try."

"A detective? That explains why your dog is named Gum Shoe."

Caleb rubbed Gum Shoe's head. "You got it."

Van yipped his approval.

"So you were working the craft fair undercover the entire time? And you work with Pierce?" I asked.

"Yes, we work together in the police department. And we had suspicions that someone was stealing from other craft fairs. When Evan and Max moved over here, we decided to come by to see if it happened again. Unfortunately, it turned deadly quickly, as you know."

"Yes, unfortunately for Evan. I'm just glad Max and

Ruth were stopped and no one else was harmed."

"I'm glad they've been arrested too. Thanks to your amateur sleuthing and your chihuahua."

"A girl and her chihuahua have to do what a girl and her chihuahua have to do," I said.

Caleb laughed.

"I can't believe I didn't know you were undercover. I should've guessed. I'm not much of a detective if I couldn't figure that out."

"Well, I like to think I'm good at my job, and that's why you didn't know." Caleb winked. "By the way, is the ghost from the painting still around?"

Elizabeth waved her arms through the air, as if guiding in a landing airplane. "I'm here."

"She's still around," I said with a smile.

Van barked and wagged his tail. When I looked to my right to see what had caught his attention, I spotted Pierce walking toward us. Pierce briefly shifted his attention to Caleb. I wanted to know what had happened between the two. Behind him, I could see the police place Ruth and Max into the back of a police cruiser.

Ruth looked right at me as she got into the back seat and said, "Your artwork is horrible."

"She's not a fan," I said as I looked at Caleb.

"I wouldn't worry about her critique," he said.

When Pierce reached us, he said, "Do you mind if I talk with Celeste for a minute?"

Caleb didn't look as if he was thrilled about the idea, but he said, "I'll see you in a bit, okay, Celeste?"

"Sure," I said.

Caleb winked at me again before smirking at Pierce. There was something obviously going on between them. I'd like to know what kind of history they had with each other.

"So, you had quite an eventful day," Pierce said.

I groaned. "Yes, you could say that."

"Caleb told you everything?" Pierce gestured toward him with a tilt of his head.

Caleb had moved over to talk to the other officers, but he glanced over at us every once in a while.

"I think he told me mostly everything that happened," I said. "Maybe not everything. I get a sense you guys don't like each other that much."

"I wouldn't say that at all," Pierce said.

Yet he didn't seem willing to give any details about why they kept giving each other looks like that. It seemed like there was some sort of competition between them. A rivalry. I suppose if they wanted to deal with that, it was none of my business.

"I was wondering if maybe now that the investigation is over, you'd want to go to dinner with me sometime?" Pierce asked.

I knew my face must've turned red because I felt the heat in my cheeks. I had hoped he would ask me that. I wanted to spend time with him and get to know him a bit better. But I immediately looked over at Caleb. It was as if he knew what Pierce was asking me. I didn't know what the right thing was to say.

"Sure, dinner sometime would be great," I croaked.

My phone rang and interrupted Pierce before he could comment. "Just a sec." I held up my index finger.

"Celeste, this is your aunt Patsy."

"Yes, I have your number programmed in my phone, Aunt Patsy. Your name comes up when you call," I said. I'd told her this before. She never remembered. So much for her claim of having a memory like an elephant.

"I remembered where I've seen Caleb. He gave me a warning for speeding a few months back. That was nice of him, right? Why didn't he tell you he was a detective?"

"I'll come by for dinner, Aunt Patsy. I have a lot to tell you."

ACKNOWLEDGMENTS

Many thanks to my family and friends. They embrace my quirkiness. Love you all! Also, thank you to my editor, Michaela Hamilton, and my agent, Jill Marsal.

Don't miss the next delightful
Haunted Craft Fair mystery!

MURDER CAN CONFUSE YOUR CHIHUAHUA

Coming soon from Kensington Publishing Corp.

Keep reading to enjoy a teaser excerpt . . .

CHAPTER 1

How would I escape this? I was trapped with no idea how to get out. Where was help when I needed it? My heart rate spiked while my body trembled.

With shaky hands, I gripped the steering wheel of my 1947 pink Ford F100 truck. I punched the gas pedal, hoping to flee before anyone noticed. Unfortunately, the wheels spun, but the truck, with my pink-and-white Shasta trailer attached to the back, went nowhere. As I gunned the engine, I wondered if I'd caused irreversible damage.

Vincent van Gogh, my sweet white chihuahua, sat on the seat next to me. He barked, as if telling me I was doing this all wrong.

"I know, Van, but what else can I do?" I pressed my foot on the pedal again.

I'd named Van after the famed artist. It wasn't

entirely because of my love of art either. I'd rescued the Chihuahua from the shelter a year ago,
and his one floppy ear had inspired the name.
We'd been best friends ever since. Van was opin-
ionated, though,. and always let me know when I
wasn't doing something to his satisfaction.

I'd been so close to arriving at my destination,
only to be stopped a short distance away. The spot
where I'd set up my booth for the annual Farewell
Summer Arts and Crafts Fair came into view. Low-
hanging clouds covered the Great Smoky Mountain-
tops in the distance. The open space for the craft fair
was surrounded by the dense green landscape, but
dots of yellow, orange, and red were forcing their
way to the surface.

This was more than a little embarrassing. Other
vendors had taken notice that I was stuck in the
mud. They stared instead of offering to help.

"I guess I should give up, huh, Van?" I released a
heavy sigh.

He barked.

Checking the rearview mirror, I caught a
glimpse of my reflection. This was not my best moment. My dark bangs stuck to my forehead with
perspiration. Actually, my grandma Judy said we
didn't sweat, we glistened. That sounded much
more ladylike. It didn't help matters that the temperature was hot enough to fry an egg on the hood
of my truck.

Late summer had settled around us, but the
heat outside held on as if not ready for a "see you
next summer." An early morning thunderstorm

had dissipated, and the sun was forcing its way out from behind the fading clouds. Steamy mist had settled over the area. Unfortunately, the mud hadn't dried up yet. Soon, the weather would change, and the green leaves would burst with color. For now, we had to deal with the scorching heat.

I was in Cherokee, North Carolina, for the craft fair. My hometown of Gatlinburg was just on the other side of the mountain. Which meant I was still close enough to go home so that my overprotective and wacky family could keep tabs on me. I expected to see them pop up at any time. Grandma Judy in her large Cadillac, my loud brothers, Stevie and Hank, my bumbling father, and my mother, who tried to keep the chaos to a tolerable level. Bless her heart.

I'd attended this fair in the past, but only as a fan. It had been almost like a county fair, with rides, games, food trailers selling deep-fried everything, and, of course, the arts and crafts. On the final day of the fair, they held a farewell picnic with hot dogs, hamburgers, and fireworks—sending the summer away with a big bang.

Pounding on the window next to me made me jump. A loud shriek escaped my lips. Caleb Ward stood beside my truck door with a perplexed grimace on his face. His sapphire-blue eyes widened. The color reminded me of the hue I used often for the sky in my paintings. I lowered the window.

"Need some help?" he asked with a slight hint of a Southern drawl.

Now I really was mortified. I hated making mistakes like this. I liked it better when I felt in control. This was definitely not being in control.

"I guess I got stuck in the mud," I said.

"Just a little." He pinched his index finger and thumb together to showcase the amount.

Heat rushed to my cheeks. "This is embarrassing."

"Nothing to be embarrassed about. Good morning, Van." Caleb waved.

Van wagged his tail. Caleb had an adorable German shepherd named Gum Shoe. For that reason, Van had become partial to Caleb. Caleb and I had met recently, at another craft fair. Not only was Caleb a talented wood sculptor, he was also a detective with the Tennessee Bureau of Investigations. Gum Shoe sat near Caleb, patiently waiting for me to get out of this predicament.

I'd rolled up to the craft fair with the best intentions. Selling my paintings was the goal. Plus, having fun with Van and enjoying nature's beautiful surroundings. Scenes like these always inspired my muse. The fact that Caleb was here too made it even better. Now, if I could only get out of this mess—literally—the day could continue as planned.

"You just need a little traction, that's all," Caleb said.

"How do we do that?" I asked.

"First put the truck in Park. Then hand me the floor mat."

I shifted the truck into Park and opened the truck door. "Stay put, Van."

After I handed Caleb the floor mat, he said, "Okay, I'm going to put this in front of the tire. When I say go, you drive forward."

"Got it," I said as I slipped back into the truck.

Van was occupied with barking at a cricket that had jumped onto the windshield. I watched in the mirror as Caleb placed the floor mat on the ground. There was no way this would help, right?

Caleb stood up and motioned. "Okay, drive forward now, slowly."

As I pushed on the gas, the truck and trailer broke free from the mud. I watched through the side mirror in horror as globs of mud splattered all over Caleb's white T-shirt and face like an erupting volcano. I bit my lip to keep from laughing. The last thing I wanted was for him to see me amused after he'd helped me out of my muddy entanglement. Once I stopped the truck, Caleb walked back to the driver's side window.

I opened the truck's door and got out. "I am so sorry."

Caleb wiped the mud from his face with his hand. "They say mud is good for the complexion, right?"

The muck had made its way into his short hair. I held back laughter until he let loose. The other vendors watched us as if we were bonkers. Caleb and I continued laughing.

I pulled a paint rag from my truck and handed it to Caleb. "Thanks again for getting us out."

Caleb swiped the towel across his face. "No problem. Do you need any help setting up?"

I took the dirty towel from his outstretched hand. "Thanks, but I think I'm good."

"I'll see you soon?" Caleb asked.

My stomach danced. "Yes, we're a couple of booths from each other."

"Guess I got lucky with that." He winked.

I blushed every time I thought of him. He wouldn't be right next to me, but he would be just a few spaces down. That meant I would see him more often. I hadn't met the vendors who would be on either side of me yet, but I hoped they were nice.

I gestured over my shoulder toward the truck. "Okay, I should get to work. See you soon."

Caleb waved as I hopped into the truck and shifted into gear. Van released his high-pitched bark, which sounded more like a cricket chirp.

"Yes, you'll get to play with Gum Shoe later."

Needless to say, the pink paint of my Shasta was now covered with mud. Yes, my trailer was pink and white, and I'd had my old truck painted pink too. Pink was my favorite color, although I loved all colors. Mostly, I just wanted everyone to remember me, and standing out with the pink was one way for that to happen. People would never forget my mobile pink art studio. My poor, dirty truck and trailer. I'd have to wash them soon or everyone would think the color was beige.

I wondered if I hadn't unknowingly selected pink as my signature color because I needed something cheerful. Sometimes the subject matter of my art wasn't so cheery. I'd recently discovered hidden images within my work. Actually, someone else had discovered this by accident, when they'd held a glass jar up to a painted canvas. That sounds crazy, but it had actually happened.

Within the paintings were images of skeletons. I

had no idea I'd painted them. I hadn't discovered the figures were there until after the paintings were complete and I held a glass up to my eye for a view. Even though this was a bit spooky, one of the images had helped me solve a recent murder. It could have been a coincidence, but I had a tough time believing that.

I maneuvered my truck and trailer closer to the spot where I'd spend the next week. Most of the area was surrounded by tall trees like a forest. The sun created flickering shadows on the ground as it trickled around the leaves. An area in the middle had lush green grass and would be the spot for the vendors to sell their crafts.

Pulling my trailer up to the location, I shoved the gearshift into Park. I had wasted almost an hour stuck in the mud, so now my setup time was limited. The craft fair would officially open for the day soon. My fingers were crossed that nothing else would go wrong at the weeklong event. There had been enough chaos at the last craft fair. I didn't want that to spill over to this one.

As I got out of the truck with Van in my arms, he whined and squirmed. "Okay, you want to go for a quick walk? We can't be long, though."

The craft fair was being held at a church that had a large area of surrounding acres, with the Oconaluftee River running along the edge of the property. They called it a river, but in this area, and at this time of year, it appeared more like a creek. My excitement mounted when I thought about spending a week here, surrounded by the lush green landscape. Oak, maple, and pine trees stood out against the bright blue, late summer sky. I thought it would be great to take my easel down to the water and paint in the early mornings before the fair started.

Van trotted along beside me as we headed down the meandering dirt path toward the river. Overgrown patches on either side of the trail gave me a creepy feeling that someone could be hiding and watching us. Van and I weaved around tall pines as the rays of sunshine trickled through the gaps in the trees. Water droplets on the leaves from the earlier thunderstorm had almost dried up completely now. The fallen needles crunched under my feet as I stepped over them. The pine scent encircled us.

Up ahead, I spotted the river. The sun sparkled off the water's surface. Gravel in shades of gray and white made up the rocky shoreline. Small waves lapped at the water's edge with knobby driftwood nearby. Trees hemmed the flow of the water. The only sound came from the rustle of the tall trees swaying with the wind, the drone of insects, and the gentle lap of the water against the shore.

"How beautiful, Van," I said.

He barked, and his four legs lifted off the ground with the motion.

"What is it, Van?" I asked as he tugged on the leash.

Obviously, he wanted me to see something. He dragged me closer to the water. I caught a glimpse of something on the ground up ahead. It was partially hidden behind one of the trees. As I drew near, I soon realized the legs on the ground were sticking out from behind the tree's trunk. Someone wearing white tennis shoes was lying there.

"Oh my gosh, Van. Someone's hurt." I scooped him up and rushed toward the person.

As soon as I came upon the woman, I knew she was more than just hurt. She was dead.

Connect with

Grab These Cozy Mysteries
from
Kensington Books

Available Wherever Books Are Sold!

All available as e-books, too!

Visit our website at **www.kensingtonbooks.com**